TAKE A CHANCE WITH ME

A WITH ME IN SEATTLE NOVEL

KRISTEN PROBY

Take a Chance With Me
A With Me In Seattle Novel
By
Kristen Proby

TAKE A CHANCE WITH ME

A With Me In Seattle Novel

Kristen Proby

Cover Design: By Hang Le

Cover photo: Wander Aguiar

Paperback ISBN: 978-1-63350-114-0

PROLOGUE

~MAGGIE~

Two Years Ago

"*I*'m gonna go talk to him." I suck down the last half of my martini, confidence bolstered by the liquor and having my friends around me. It's a girls' night out in my family's pub, and damn it, I need...*something*.

A connection? Attention from a man that my piece-of-shit late husband was never willing—or able—to provide, perhaps?

A damn orgasm for the first time in my life.

All of the above.

I slide out of the booth and take a deep breath. If I don't go over to the bar and talk to him now, I never will. And damn it, he's *hot*.

Of course, if my eldest brother, Kane, finds out, he might be super mad at me. I'm about to hit on his best friend, after all. And, well, that's just madness. Cameron Cox has been in my life for as long as I can remember. He's a decade older than me, so I don't know him well. He's just always...*there.*

And he's the sexiest man on the planet.

I'm drunk. I'm sick of being sad and embarrassed. And I want him.

"Hey," I say as I sidle up next to him at the bar. Keegan, my other brother, raises a brow, asking if I want a drink, but I shake my head. He tips his lips in a half-grin and walks off to help other customers.

Cameron's gaze turns down to me, and he smiles.

Fucking hell, his smile should be illegal in the presence of a slightly drunk woman.

"Hi, yourself," he says. "You doing okay?"

It's now or never, Mags. Let's do this.

"Honestly? I'm great. But I could use some company, if you know what I mean. *Naked* company."

That smile vanishes, and his crystal-blue eyes narrow on me. His jaw tightens. My heart beats so hard that blood rushes through my ears, drowning out everything else around me.

If he turns me away right now, I might die of embarrassment.

He shakes his head, sips his beer as if he's trying to come up with a response—or an excuse—and then pins me with that intense gaze once more.

"I'm not one to turn down an offer like that from the most gorgeous woman here."

I laugh in relief and lay my hand on his shoulder, which he takes and kisses. And then, without another word, we walk out of the bar.

He leads me to his car, a classic Mustang, but before he opens the passenger door, he leans in and whispers in my ear.

"Are you absolutely sure this is what you want, Maggie?"

"Yes." *Absolutely. Give me all the orgasms.*

"It could open a can of worms with the family," he warns me.

"I'm an adult, Cam. I get to make these decisions for myself. Unless you're afraid of Kane."

"Kane doesn't scare me." He sighs and drags a thumb down my cheek. "And you're not just sad or angry?"

I know he's asking if I'm coming on to him because of grief after losing my husband a month ago. But I'm not grieving. He was mean to me, didn't love me, and made me feel worthless.

"No, this isn't grief talking."

He nods, kisses my cheek, and opens the door. "Fair enough."

I sit in the low seat and take another deep breath. The cool Washington air helped to clear my head a bit, but I'm still floaty, my lips a little numb as he sits next to me and fires up the engine. Without asking, he drives us to his hotel, the place he stays whenever he's in town, and again takes me by the hand to lead me up to his suite.

His hand is big, firm, and folds around mine with a comforting warmth I didn't expect. He's tall, muscular, and lean through the hips.

I've wanted to bury my fingers in his thick, dark hair for years. And when alone and lying in the dark, I often wondered what his lips would taste like.

Not that I would have ever acted on it. Not in a million years. He's my brother's best friend, and I was married.

But now, I'm not.

When we're in the room, and the door is closed, Cameron rounds on me, pins my back to the wood, and lowers his head to mine. He presses his lips to my forehead, my nose, and then glides them over to my ear, sending a thrilling chill down my arms.

"Gorgeous," he whispers, echoing his sentiment in the bar. "Fucking amazing."

My breath catches when he skims his teeth over my skin, just beneath my ear. His hands push up under my shirt, over my ribs.

Nothing in my entire twenty-six years has ever made me feel like *this.*

"If you want me to stop," he whispers before nipping at my jawline, "just tell me to, okay?"

I nod, but he pulls back to look into my eyes and takes my chin in his fingers.

"Use your words, Maggie." I like that he's in control. That he's taking care of me and is so sure of himself.

"I understand." My voice is squeaky and broken, and his lips pull into a small smile.

Those magical hands of his glide back down to cup my ass, and the next thing I know, he's lifting me against him. With my arms wrapped around his neck, he carries me to the bed and lays me down.

The first kiss is staggering. If I were on my feet, I'd fall to the floor. His lips are soft and sure, not bruising or aggressive.

They tease open my mouth, and he takes his time. Truly just sinks in and leisurely kisses and touches and learns.

He presses one leg between mine, just over the most intimate part of me that begs for more, denim against denim, and I feel the flush move through me from my head to my feet.

My hands slide into his hair as he takes the kiss deeper, and we start to move against each other, searching for more.

"Skin," I gasp as I grapple with his shirt. "I want your clothes off."

"Excellent idea." He pushes up onto his knees and tugs his shirt over his head, dropping it onto the floor. In the moonlight, I can see his chiseled muscles. His smooth flesh. I can't help but reach out to touch him, letting my fingertips dance over his skin.

"Am I dreaming this?" He smiles, and I realize that I spoke the thought aloud.

"If you are, don't wake us up," he says as he helps me out of my shirt and bra. The next thing I know, his lips are around my nipple, and my hips are moving, grinding against his leg.

God, I want him. I don't think I've ever wanted anything more. And if the amazing sensations moving through me are any indication, I'll be getting some long-overdue orgasms very soon.

He easily unfastens my jeans and pushes his hand inside, under my panties. When he finds my center, he groans.

"Christ, you're slick," he whispers and bites my chin.

I spread my legs wider in invitation, and he slides a finger inside me.

"Oh, God." I arch my back, and he licks my nipple as his hand does magical things between my legs. Just as I'm about to come, he pulls his hand away. "No, don't stop, Cameron."

"Not yet," he replies and kisses me again. "I want you to come when I'm inside you."

"Then get a move on, damn it."

He laughs and pushes his jeans down his hips, reaching for a condom. But before he can rip the packet open, his phone rings.

We still and stare at each other in the moonlight.

"Don't answer it."

"I have to. It's my job, Maggie."

I shake my head, but he reaches over and, with his eyes pinned to mine, answers.

"Cox." His eyes narrow. "Copy that. What's the ETA? Damn. Yeah, yeah, I've got it. On my way."

He hangs up and tosses his phone onto the bed, then looks down at me with an apology written all over his face.

"No."

"I'm sorry, I have to go." He kisses me lightly. "I have to be at the airstrip in twenty minutes."

You have got to be kidding me!

"Don't leave me like this. Call in sick or something."

"That's not how this works." His expression is grim as he tugs me close to him. "I'm sorry, Maggie. I'll make it up to you."

I'll make it up to you.

I've heard those words before. More times than I can count.

"Forget about it." I reach for my shirt and tug it over my head. "This was probably a bad idea anyway."

He fastens his jeans and pulls his shirt on, his hair a mess as he stares at me with conflict waging war in his blue eyes.

"This isn't over. As soon as I'm able, I'll be back, Maggie."

"Where are you going?"

"I can't tell you that."

"Right." I nod and blow out a breath. "You'd better go."

"You're mad."

"Bet your ass, I'm mad. But we don't have time to get into that now."

He crosses to me and cups my face, but I've already emotionally pulled away.

Men leave. They lie. Break promises and leave me hanging.

I knew better than this. I don't know why I thought it would be different with Cam.

Cameron kisses me softly. "I promise, I'll be back. Do you want me to drive you to the pub?"

"No." Hell, no. I'd rather die. "I'm good. Don't worry about me."

He throws some things into his bag, looks back at me once more, and then he's gone.

And I know in my heart that I'll never be able to forgive him for this—or myself for letting it happen. Even if it's not entirely Cameron's fault. I know he has a job that takes him away, but it's too familiar, too close to what I put up with from the jerk I was married to.

Cameron is the *last* man on the planet I should be throwing myself at.

And I'd do well to remember that.

CHAPTER 1

~MAGGIE~

"For the love of all that's holy, it's blustery out there," I announce and shiver as I hurry into the pub, just a little late for my shift. I'm on table duty, and despite the monsoon outside, it'll be a busy Saturday night in the bar, full of regulars and tourists alike, taking refuge from the storm. "Sorry, I'm late. My car was giving me fits."

"Mary Margaret, you need a new vehicle," Keegan says as I wiggle out of my rain slicker. "You've needed one for years."

"I don't drive very much." I can hear the defensiveness in my voice. "Just here and home. The store once in a while. It does fine."

My brother looks as if he wants to disagree, but I shake my head at him.

"It's fine," I repeat and grab a clean black apron, tying it around my waist. "What do you want to wager that the customers won't have the sense to stay home and out of this mess?"

"I hope they don't," Keegan says with a laugh. "We need them, lass."

"How are Izzy and the baby?"

I swear, I'm surrounded by babies these days. Between Keegan and Izzy and Kane and Anastasia, we have two little ones about, and my sister, Maeve, is halfway through her first pregnancy.

We're just a baby factory around here.

Keegan's face softens into a gooey smile. Never thought I'd see the day that I would describe my brother as *gooey*, but here we are. He's completely and utterly smitten with his gorgeous wife and their newborn daughter. It's fun to watch.

"They're the sun and stars," he says. "And doing well. Izzy's overseeing some things at the new house."

"When do you move in? I thought it was done. Also, how you managed to build a house in less than a year, I'll never know. Construction crews have been short-handed the past couple of years, slowing everything down."

"We were lucky, and that's the truth of it. Izzy wants things to be just so before we move in so we don't have to do any work with the house once we're in. I can't blame her. She has her hands full with the baby, as well."

Izzy hasn't wanted any of us to come to the new

house, not until it's all furnished and ready so she can have a grand reveal. I'm dying to see it.

We O'Callaghans are a tight-knit bunch, we know everything about each other, and it's unheard of for us *not* to be involved in a project from start to finish.

But it'll be a fun housewarming party when Izzy decides she's ready.

"Good God, it's a mess out there," Maeve announces as she walks inside. She has Rachel, her new step-daughter, with her. Rachel's been working for us for a while now, clearing tables and delivering food orders, and I don't know what we'd do without her. "I guess the rainy season is upon us. Again."

"I made an extra pot of stew," I say as I wipe off my tray and get ready to wait tables. "It'll go fast in this weather."

"Brilliant," Keegan says just as the door opens and a table of four walks inside. "Here we go."

Despite the moody early spring weather, the customers are jovial and happy to be out of the rain. The Guinness flows, hot food from the kitchen is dispatched thanks to my brother Shawn and his wife, Lexi, and the night moves on without a hitch.

"I need two pints of Guinness and a cola, please," I say to Keegan and wait for him to fill the drink order as Maeve approaches and calls out her order, as well. Despite being in her second trimester, the woman can *move*. And she never complains. "Was that guy bothering you?"

I noticed a man in his thirties with bright copper hair giving my sister a toothy grin. He was a little too friendly for my taste.

We've seen all kinds in here. Been groped and slapped. Even had to hit back and kick them out a couple of times. Press charges.

Thankfully, that's rare, but it's not unheard of.

"Nah, he's harmless," she says, waving off my concern. "So, what's up with you? Are you going to see Mr. Pickup Truck again?"

I roll my eyes at the thought of Monday's date.

"No. Turns out he's still legally married." I sigh and lean on the bar. "Online dating is hard. Why are so many people horrible?"

"If I knew the answer to that, I'd be rich," Maeve replies.

"You *are* rich."

"My husband's rich," she retorts. As a former MMA fighting superstar, Hunter has more money than God himself. "I'm not rich."

"Whatever." I roll my eyes and shake my head at my stubborn sister. "And to answer your question about Mr. Pickup Truck, no, that idiot isn't allowed to speak to me again. We got halfway into dinner when he casually mentioned that not only is he still legally married, but he also *lives* with his wife and two kids."

"So, he's just plain *married*," Maeve says.

"Exactly. What a jerk. But I am going to dinner

tomorrow night with a guy who says he just moved here to the island. I don't have high hopes."

"Where are you going?"

"I'm meeting him at the diner. Easy, casual, and no one should be able to screw this up. Then we'll take it from there."

"Good plan."

Maeve's gaze leaves my face and focuses on something just over my shoulder. When I turn around, I find Cameron Cox standing right behind me.

I freaking *hate* the way my body comes alive when I see him. How I immediately remember what it was like to be half-naked and in his arms—and then frustrated and embarrassed when he abandoned me.

The jerk.

"Hi." I hear the moodiness in my voice that always appears when Cameron's near.

"Hey, yourself. So, going on a date tomorrow, huh?"

"Yeah." I load my tray and, without sparing him another look, set off to my tables. I deliver drinks and take food orders. I joke with my regular customers and sing along with the band as I weave my way through the tables.

All the while, I'm acutely aware of Cam's gaze following me through the pub.

We've had moments alone since that night. He's been a good friend.

But that's all he'll ever be. A friend. Because he doesn't *stay*. And I've been in that relationship. I've been alone while my husband goes off to God knows where. I'm not doing that again.

But when I return to the bar and see Cam's blue gaze on mine, I feel that flutter in my belly that I always do. I still want him.

I just can't have him.

"So, you work at that Irish pub in town?"

My date's name is Derek Lewis, and when he saw the menu here at the little diner in town, he wrinkled his nose.

Apparently, Derek is vegan, and there's pretty much nothing on this greasy-spoon menu that looks appetizing to him.

His eating preferences don't bother me, but it's a *diner*.

"I do," I reply and set my napkin in my lap. I'm excited to eat the cheeseburger that's on its way out to me. "It's a family business. My brother owns it—"

"So, you don't own it?" he interrupts.

"No, my brother—"

"What are your ambitions for your career then?"

Okay, Derek is a bit of an asshole. I sit back as the waitress sets a big plate in front of me with my burger and a small mountain of fries. Derek ordered the dinner salad.

Before I can dig into my meal, I see Cameron come into the diner with a woman I don't recognize.

I narrow my eyes.

Cam looks my way, gives me a slight nod, and then sits with his date, three tables over, right in my line of sight.

Great.

"Maggie?"

"What? Oh. I'm sorry, what were you saying?"

"What do you have planned for your career? You can't work in a bar forever."

I pop a fry into my mouth and study Derek. He's in his mid-thirties with a little gray at the temples. He has a bit of acne on his chin and a crooked nose. It looks as if someone hauled off and punched him at some point, and he never had it fixed.

Frankly, I wouldn't mind punching him myself.

"Why do you say that?" I take a big bite of my burger and watch as Derek's nose wrinkles. The fact that I'm pleased by his repulsion of my food choice probably makes me a bad person.

I'm not sorry.

"Because that's not ambitious. How will you support yourself?"

"I haven't had a problem so far."

Okay, so I can't afford that new car I need, but my bills are paid, and I'm not hurting. I'm a simple girl.

Cameron laughs across the room and smiles intimately with his date, and I take another big bite of my burger.

Is he doing it on purpose? Is he trying to make me jealous? Because it's not working.

Cam reaches over and wipes something off his date's lip, and I have to fight the urge to go over there.

This is ridiculous.

"So, you're telling me that you have no intention to better yourself?"

I turn my attention back to my date and narrow my eyes at him as I feel my Irish temper starting to heat up.

"What do *you* do, Derek?"

"I'm a banker."

"Ah, so you just sit around and count *other* people's money all day."

His jaw tightens. "No, I open accounts and help people with loan applications."

"Groundbreaking." I slather a fry with ketchup and pop it into my mouth. "What are *your* aspirations?"

Cameron laughs again, and my stomach lurches, so I take another big bite of my burger.

"I'll eventually move up in the bank, and I'd like a family. A wife who also has a strong work ethic in an acceptable career. A couple of children. A home."

"If your wife is working her ass off in an *acceptable career*, who's taking care of the kids?"

"You notice I said, 'a strong work ethic.' She'll be able to handle it."

I nod and watch as Cam pays his check,—I guess they only wanted coffee?—and they walk out.

"I think it's safe to say that I won't be that wife," I say and finish my burger.

"I don't know, you're pretty enough. I'm sure you could take business courses or something and work in an office."

"Here's a little something about me, Derek." I crook my finger as if I want him to get closer so I can tell him a secret. "I was married to an asshole once already. I won't be making that mistake again. I hope you *don't* find some poor girl that you can control and mold into your idea of the perfect wife."

I toss a twenty on the table because I'll be damned if this man will pay for my dinner, and then I stand and, without a look back, stroll out of the restaurant.

I walk toward home. It's not far, and the weather cleared after our huge storm yesterday, leaving the air cool but not unpleasant.

Not to mention, my car wouldn't start again.

I've had that car for years. Joey bought it, and he was horrible about getting it serviced. He always claimed to forget, but the truth is, he just didn't care. I got stranded more than once, always to the dismay of my family, who had to come and get me. Not because they minded helping me out, but because my husband was a big jerk who didn't take care of me.

After he died, I found out that Joey had a couple of

million dollars hidden from me in different bank accounts all over the United States.

And every one listed a young girl and her mother as the beneficiary.

His daughter.

A baby he had with a woman *after* he married me.

That was a hard pill to swallow.

Joey left me with nothing. No money, a shitty car, and very little dignity.

And despite what dickhead-Derek said, I worked my ass off to come out the other side of that in one piece. I have a good job, a great family and friends, and, thanks to that family, a good home.

I make the mortgage payments, but Kane pulled me aside and told me he was making the down payment, and I wasn't about to argue.

He would have just bought it for me outright, without thinking twice. Family helps family, and Kane and I have a special relationship. We always have. I love him so much.

But I'm an adult, and I *want* to make my own way. I work hard, and I'm proud of the life I've built. I may not be wealthy, and my job may seem small to people like Derek, but I like it. I'm happy at the pub.

I get to the end of the street and sigh.

I could turn right and go home, or I could turn left and go to Cameron's house. Which would be completely stupid. He's probably with that girl.

I have no right to be upset over that idea.

No right at all.

But I turn left and head toward the house that Maeve helped him buy a few months ago. My sister not only works at the pub, she's also a real estate agent.

And a damn good one.

The house is only two blocks down, and I slow my steps as I get closer.

I'm just making an ass out of myself, and I've done enough of that where Cameron is concerned. What if he's naked with that girl? Maybe they're at *her* house.

But I can see that his car is parked in his driveway, and the porch light is on.

I stand on the sidewalk and stare at the porch, then start to pace back and forth.

What am I going to say? *Hey, I'm mad at you, but I don't want you to date other girls.*

"No, that's dumb."

I don't even know why I'm here. I should turn around and go home before Cam realizes I'm out here.

"Are you going to come inside?"

Too late.

I freeze, then turn to find Cameron on his porch, leaning against a white column, his arms crossed over his chest.

"I haven't decided."

He nods and waits while I return to pacing.

Damn him! Why does he have to look so smug? So damn hot? Why can't I just forget about that night with him and move on with my life as if nothing happened?

"It's a little chilly out here," he says and looks up at the darkening sky. "Might rain."

"You can go back inside. Won't hurt my feelings." And then I can have my existential crisis by myself.

"I'll wait."

I sigh and realize that my fingers and nose *are* cold.

There's no harm in going inside to warm up.

"Fine. I'll come in."

I climb the stairs, and a slow smile spreads over Cameron's lips as I get closer to him. He gestures for me to go inside ahead of him.

"If you have company, I can leave."

"No one's here but you and me." His voice is calm. Mild. Friendly.

And, damn it, he looks amazing in that tight T-shirt and jeans that hug his hips in just the right way. I *know* what's under those clothes and how he feels. How he smells.

This was a huge mistake.

"So, did you have a nice date?" I blurt out. I can't even turn and look at him, so I walk to the window and stare outside. I have all these emotions swirling inside, and I don't know what to do with them.

"Maggie."

"Did you do it on purpose?" I turn and stare at him, propping my hands on my hips. "You overheard me telling Maeve last night that I'd be at the diner, so you paraded some tramp in there to make me jealous, right?"

"Actually, no." He shoves his hands into his pockets. "I'd already made the date—with a *client*—a few weeks ago."

"So, you're dating, then."

He narrows his eyes. "I just said she's a client. But let's set that aside for a second. You're dating, too."

Damn it, Mary Margaret, stop this! You sound like a fool.

He looks frustrated. Cam's always calm and collected, so I've clearly gotten him worked up. His voice is firm but quiet as he asks, "How did it go with *your* date?"

"Oh, he's a moron." I wave that off and pace back to the window, feeling completely mortified. "He's a misogynistic, basic asshole."

"So, you didn't like him then?"

I can't help but chuckle. "No. I didn't like him."

"Why are you here, Maggie?"

I don't turn around. I don't want him to see the hurt on my face. Damn it, why does this whole thing hurt my feelings? He just said the bimbo at the diner was a client.

"I was in the neighborhood."

I feel him walk up behind me and rest his hands on my shoulders. "Mary Margaret."

"I was just in the neighborhood," I repeat and pull away from him, angry all over again. At him, at myself for letting him get under my skin. "Good for you for going on dates, even if the girl obviously has fake boobs."

"What's wrong with you?" He raises his voice, and that's something I've never heard from Cameron before.

"Nothing." I march to the front door, but Cam stops me before I can reach for the knob.

"You've made it clear to me that I don't have a chance in hell with you, Maggie." His voice is raised, full of frustration and anger. "I've tried, damn it. I'm your friend, and I will be forever, but you've established that that's all it is for us. You can't even fucking *look* at me."

"You left me!" I round on him, the anger spilling out of me so fast, I couldn't have stopped it if I'd tried. "You embarrassed me. And, damn it, I've had it up to my eyeballs with men who do that shit to me. I won't have it. I. Will. Not. Have. It!"

"Don't you dare lump me in with that fuckup you married."

"Why not?" I lean in closer to him. "You acted just like him. Worse, actually, because I *cared* when you took off, and I never did when he left."

"Mags." He reaches for me, but I back out of his grasp and shake my head.

"Forget it." I hold up my hands in surrender. "This was obviously a horrible idea, and it was dumb to come here. I don't know what I was trying to accomplish or prove. Good luck with Fake Boobs."

Before he can say anything else, I hurry out of the house and run down the stairs, walking toward my house, my feet moving swiftly.

Jesus, why do I always embarrass myself with that man? What is it about him that has me continuously making a fool of myself? Did I think I'd catch him in the act with that chick? And then what?

I'm ridiculous, and I need to get over him. Cameron will always be a part of our family, so I'll see him from time to time.

That's fact.

I just wish I didn't feel pulled to him as if he's meant to be mine when it's perfectly clear that that's not the case at all.

And I really need to stop letting my temper take over. That's what gets me into these messes.

Instead, I need to take a deep breath, count to ten, and then walk away.

Man, I'm an idiot.

CHAPTER 2

~CAMERON~

I'd like to spank her ass.

Just throw her over my knee and paddle her. I didn't sleep at all last night and had to stop myself from marching down to her house and having it out with her several times. When she's all fired up, and in a temper, it doesn't do any good to try to reason with her.

I love her fiery personality, but it frustrates the hell out of me.

If I weren't completely and utterly in love with her, I'd walk away. Be content with being her eldest brother's best friend, and that's it.

But I've had a thing for Maggie since I came back to town when she was about twenty, and I discovered that she'd grown up into a gorgeous, interesting woman.

Unfortunately, she was already married to the asshole who would eventually try to destroy her.

We all knew Joey was an idiot, and no one liked how he spoke to Maggie when we were around. I can only imagine what it was like for her when we *weren't* around. Until he died, she didn't say much about it. After he had the heart attack, we learned that he'd been cheating for years.

What a complete moron.

I should have made her stay put last night. Made her listen. But it's not easy to make Maggie do anything she doesn't want to do.

It's one of the things I love about her.

I'll go find her later this morning and smooth things over. She might have an Irish temper, but she doesn't stay angry for long.

I rinse my coffee mug and set it in the sink. Grabbing my keys, I open the front door and then stop short.

"That's twice in less than twenty-four hours I've found you outside my house."

Maggie's on the steps, her back to me. She sits up tall when she hears my voice. I walk over and lower myself next to her. She's in a puffy orange jacket with a gray hat over her red hair. She's holding a pink box and has two cups sitting on the step next to her sneaker-clad feet.

"I brought you coffee and donuts," she whispers. "Because I'm a jerk, and I need to apologize."

"You're not a jerk, Mags."

"Yeah, I am." She shrugs a shoulder and finally turns

her sweet face to me. She has tears in her gorgeous green eyes. "I'm sorry I'm a moron."

"If you don't stop calling yourself names, I'm gonna get really mad." I lean over and kiss her cheek. "What kind of donuts did you bring?"

"French crullers."

"Those are my favorite."

"I know." She passes the box over to me and then grabs one of the cups, offering me that, as well. "And coffee. Black."

"You should yell at me more often. I get good food out of it."

"It's not funny." She sounds miserable, and I want to pull her to me and hold her close. Reassure her.

But I don't know if that would be welcome.

I stand with the treats in my hands and motion for her to follow me. "Come on inside. I can't eat these all by myself."

"Weren't you headed out somewhere?"

"Yeah, to find you. Come inside, Maggie."

She stands, and with her coffee clutched in her hands, walks inside behind me.

"It's damn cold out there," she says with a shiver.

"How long were you sitting on my stoop?"

"Only about a half hour or so. I didn't want to wake you up or anything."

I turn and stare at her. "A *half hour?* For Christ's sake, Maggie, you'll catch a cold."

"That's an old wives' tale," she says and then promptly sneezes. Her eyes widen, and she points at me. "That was a coincidence."

I laugh, open the pink box, and eat one of the crullers in two bites, then reach for another. "They're still warm."

"You're so classy," she says with an eye roll as I shove another into my mouth. Suddenly, I know that last night's storm has passed. "Why were you coming to see me?"

I wash the donut down with a sip of coffee and lean on the counter as Maggie sits on a stool at the kitchen island and nibbles on a donut. I like seeing her in my place. I just like having her nearby, period.

"I was coming to talk about last night."

She sighs. "I was afraid of that. Can we forget it ever happened? Because I know I was acting foolish and rash. And you're allowed to date anyone you like—it's not really any of my business."

I narrow my eyes and cross my arms over my chest so I don't just yank her against me and kiss the hell out of her.

"Did you not hear me last night when I told you that the woman was a freaking *client?*"

"I heard you."

"But you didn't believe me."

She shrugs a shoulder again. "I have no reason *not* to believe you."

"Jesus, you're the most frustrating woman on the damn planet."

"Well, I apologized, so I'll just leave now if I'm that bleeding frustrating."

"You'll sit your ass on that stool, Mary Margaret."

Her eyes widen at my tone, and I swear under my breath. "You'd test the patience of a saint."

"And you're no saint," she says. "I guess I forget that sometimes. Because you're always so calm and collected. You never get worked up."

"I do, too. Especially when it comes to you."

"I'm not sure if that's a compliment."

"Me, either."

Her lips twitch into the first signs of a smile. "I really am sorry that I overreacted yesterday. It was silly."

"Your feelings were hurt." I sip my coffee and watch as a frown creases her brow as if she doesn't want to admit that her feelings were, in fact, bruised last night. "And I need to apologize for that. I didn't mean to hurt you, Mags."

She opens and closes her mouth and then settles on that frown again. "It was silly to get worked up."

"I wanted to break that asshole's arm."

Her head whips up in surprise. "Whose?"

"The jerk that you were out with. He looked smarmy, and I only saw him from behind."

She laughs and nods in agreement, biting her donut.

"Yeah, he was a piece of work. He thinks I should have a better career plan than just working at the pub for the rest of my life. And he was sorely disappointed that I don't own the place."

"Maybe I'll hunt him down anyway. Punch out some teeth."

She giggles, and my gut clenches. God, I love her laugh.

"I basically told him to go fuck himself."

"Good girl."

She swallows hard and frowns down at her coffee cup.

"You said something last night that's stuck with me," she says. "That you've tried to have more with me, but I've made it clear that we're only friends."

I just lift a brow and wait for her to continue.

"It's not because I don't like you or find you attractive. I mean, that should be pretty obvious."

"Nothing is obvious with you, Mary Margaret."

"I *threw* myself at you, Cameron."

"Yeah, almost two years ago. And you've barely tolerated me since."

"I—" She stops and folds her lips in, frowning. "It messed me up when you left."

"I didn't have a choice," I begin and then stop when her green eyes flash. "Okay. I'm sorry."

"You're a sexy, intelligent, and fun guy, Cameron, but you don't stay. You're in and out constantly, and I was married to that before. It fucked me up, and that's just not what I want in a relationship."

"I bought this house," I say quietly and glance around the white kitchen. "I quit my job."

Her mouth drops open in surprise.

"Your brothers didn't tell you?"

"I knew you bought the house, but I didn't know about your job."

"I work from here now. I might have to travel occasionally, but it shouldn't be more than a couple of times a year. This is my home base. My office. I have a pretty sweet setup upstairs."

"I want to see it."

I mentally scan the room to make sure there isn't anything confidential out in the open that she can't see, and then crook my finger and lead her up the stairs.

"What do you do for a living?" she asks. "Whenever I ask anyone, they just tell me that we aren't allowed to know."

"And you're still not allowed to know most of it," I confirm when I open the door to my office and gesture for her to walk in. "What I do is highly classified."

"With the government?"

"Sometimes."

She blows out a breath and stares at the bookshelves and the blank computer screens on my desk.

"I can't do secrets," she says at last. "It's a hard limit for me, Cam."

"A *hard limit?*" I grin. "I'd like to know what your other hard limits are."

"I'm being serious."

"So am I. Look, I can*not* tell you about the inner workings of my job. I could go to jail for talking about it. I mostly work with computers and databases."

Her eyes narrow. "You're a computer geek?"

"Why does that surprise you?"

"Because you're way too hot to be a geek."

"So, you think I'm hot?"

She rolls her eyes again, but I see the flush on her cheeks. The attraction isn't one-sided here at all.

And I'm enjoying the hell out of her. It's the first time since that damn night two years ago that I can see some hope here.

"I can tell you that I won't ever lie to you," I continue, and when she turns back to me, I cup the side of her face in my hand, brushing my thumb over the apple of her cheek. "If I can't talk about something because of my job, I'll say so. I'm not a liar."

"This is probably a mistake," she whispers, her eyes on my lips.

"Does it feel like a mistake?"

She bites her lip, shaking her head. "No, and that's the most frustrating part of all. I was so mad at you. So damn mad. But I just can't seem to stop thinking about you."

I kiss her forehead and breathe her in. "Let's just

start slow. Since you're hell-bent on dating, why don't *we* go on a date?"

She leans back and snorts. "Right. You want to take me on a date?"

"Why is that so hard to believe?"

"I don't know. You're...*you.* You're practically family. And you want to *date*?"

"If you have a hard time wrapping your pretty head around the idea of dating me, how can you even consider getting naked with me?"

"Because—" She stops, then blinks. "I don't know. I guess I hadn't thought about it."

"Look, as sexy as you are, and as much as I want you, I'm not interested in just sex with you, Mags."

"What are you interested in?"

I lean in, kissing her cheek. "More."

"What does that mean?"

"You have a lot of questions, don't you?"

"I always do. Drives everyone bonkers."

I chuckle and brush my hand down her soft hair. "Let's just see where this takes us for now. Go out, hang out, and let it evolve organically."

"Huh." She nods slowly. "Okay, I guess. I probably have my defenses up, and I don't mean to. That means I'll probably screw it all up."

I kiss her just to get her to stop talking. Soft, chaste, but enough to make her brain quiet, even if it's just for a minute.

"Don't overthink it," I suggest when I pull back. "Everything's going to be okay."

"Right. Unless I *do* screw it up, and then it's just weird between us at family gatherings and stuff."

"You just can't help it, can you?"

"Nope."

"Well, we've survived the weirdness between us so far."

She wrinkles her nose. "That's not encouraging."

"Don't sweat it." I drape my arm around her shoulders. "It's going to be great. When's your next night off?"

"Thursday."

"I'll pick you up at five. We'll be going into Seattle."

"For dinner?"

"To start."

"Do I need to dress fancy?"

"Nope."

She nods, and I keep her hand in mine as we walk down the steps.

"Can I take a donut with me?"

"I guess."

"Dude, I brought you a *dozen.*"

"Exactly, so it's a sacrifice to give up one of them. But I'll do it. For you. And don't tell your brother that I have them because he'll come and steal them."

"Kane's never stolen donuts in his life."

"Oh, he has."

She laughs and shakes her head. "Fine, your secret is

safe with me. I have to go get some stuff done before I head into the pub to help with inventory in a couple of hours."

"Have a good day." I tug her in so I can hug her close. God, I'll never get used to feeling her against me.

She's fucking amazing.

"You have a good day, too. Doing whatever it is you do up there. Espionage or something, right?"

I laugh and open the door for her. "Or something."

I'm GOING to do this right.

I called a meeting with Maggie's siblings and asked them to meet me at Kane's place. It's where we always go when we need to get something off our chests.

I love these people. I couldn't love them more if they were mine by blood. They're the only family I have.

And I'm not going to fuck this up.

"I'm here," Maeve announces as she hurries back to Kane's sunroom, where the rest of us just gathered. "Sorry, I just left a showing."

"We just sat down," Kane assures her, then turns to me. "What's up, man?"

I take a deep breath and wipe the palms of my hands on my jeans. "I want to date your sister."

Everyone's quiet for a moment, and then they glance at each other.

"That's it?" Shawn asks.

"Yeah. That's what I came here to talk about."

"Given that she's not here, I assume you haven't talked with *her* about it," Keegan says.

"I spoke with her this morning. I'm taking her out on Thursday. But, damn it, you're my family. I don't want to do something you hate."

"If we told you that we didn't want you to do this, would you call it off?" Kane asks.

"Yes. I wouldn't like it, but I would."

Maeve grins and rubs her little, round belly. "It's about damn time, Cam."

"I thought you'd be sixty and still pining away for her," Keegan agrees.

"Wait, you're okay with this?"

"You're both adults," Kane says. "And you're the best mate I've ever had. If it's my sister that you want, who are we to say no? As long as you treat her the way she should be treated, we've no problem with it, Cam."

"There's been something brewing between you two for a long while," Shawn adds. "We've all seen it, watched it. She snaps at you more than she smiles at you, and that's telling."

"How romantic," I mutter and pull my hand down my face. "Damn you all. I was nervous."

"You should be," Keegan replies. "Because if you fuck this up, we'll kill you and make it look like an accident."

They all smile at me.

"She was hurt once before," I reply slowly, measuring my words. "Because she was with a man who didn't love her. Who didn't appreciate her and didn't give a shit about anything but himself. That's not who I am."

"It isn't, no," Kane says.

"I don't know where it will go, to be honest with you. But, damn it, I want to try. I want to spend time with her, indulge her, spoil her a bit. I know that she has all of you, but she deserves to know what it feels like to be with someone who's crazy about her."

"You're right," Maeve says and stands to wrap her arms around me, kissing my cheek. "She does. And I'm glad that you finally realized that you're the man to do it."

"I've known for a while, but it wasn't the right time. It is now. Damn it, I don't want to stay away from her anymore."

"Then don't," Kane says simply and claps his hand on my shoulder. "She's not fragile. She's a good woman, and it's a lucky man you are if she's decided to give you her attention."

"She brought me donuts this morning."

My friend's brows shoot up in surprise. "And you didn't save me any, did you, you selfish bastard?"

"Hell, no. Your girl bakes, get your own donuts."

"I see how this is going to be," Kane says, but there's laughter in his eyes. "It's happy I am that you're after my sister. She's a good lass, and you both deserve happiness."

"I'm not marrying her."

They all raise their eyebrows, and I can't help but laugh.

"Not yet, at least. She's not ready for that."

"Are you?" Shawn asks.

"I'd marry her tomorrow. But she's still wary. We're going to take it slow."

"That's the right way to go," Maeve says and then looks around when everyone laughs. "What?"

"You didn't take your time with Hunter," Kane says.

"None of you took it slow," I remind them, but then look at Shawn. "Well, you might have been a little slow on the uptake, now that I think about it."

"I got there in the end," he says with a shrug. "It'll go at the pace that works for the both of you."

"If it's our blessing you were looking for, I'd say you have it," Keegan says.

"Yeah, I guess that's what I wanted. Thanks."

"Where are you taking her on Thursday?" Maeve wants to know.

"Seattle. We're getting off this island for a few hours to be anonymous and have a good time."

"Good for you," Kane says. "You know, you didn't have to come to us about this. We wouldn't have said no."

"Yeah, I did. Like I said, you're my family, and Maggie's

been through it. I needed to make sure that you're okay with me seeing her. Because I won't get started with her and then give her up. I know I can't do that."

"We've watched you change your life around this past year," Shawn says. "And we all suspected it was for Maggie. Love is written all over your face when you look at her."

"It's really sappy," Keegan adds, giving me a hard time. "So go after the girl already."

CHAPTER 3

~MAGGIE~

*L*ighting? Check. Phone in the holder thing? Yes.

"Let's get this done in one take today, okay?" I pace the room and blow raspberries through my lips, loosening up. No one in the family knows that I do this. It's just a little side thing that's fun. Different.

I love to sing.

And I've found a social media outlet for said singing.

Not to mention, three million viewers seem to enjoy the songs.

I like to sing Irish ballads with candles lit. It's just me and the camera in the bathroom because that's where I get the best acoustics. I've learned that one-minute songs get the most views, but sometimes I post a three-minute piece if I get carried away.

I turn off the overhead light. In the glow of the

candles, I press record and begin to sing about a love lost at sea. I turn up the Irish lilt just a bit, even though I don't have any accent at all, and thirty seconds into the song, the phone stops recording, interrupted by a call.

"Bugger it," I mutter, frustrated because that was going to be a great take.

I press the button to answer the call. "Hello?"

"Please don't hang up," a woman says, and I furrow my brow. I don't recognize her voice.

"Who is this?"

"I'm Heather Fisher. I just—"

I hang up, ball my hands into fists, and back away until I hit the wall behind me.

My mouth is suddenly dry.

"Shit," I whisper and clench my eyes closed. "Shit, shit, shit."

I won't be able to sing now, so I flip the light on, blow out the candles, and take my phone out of the stand. As I stomp out of the bathroom, I call my sister.

Maeve answers on the third ring. "Hey there. You have perfect timing. I was just leaving a showing down the street from you. What's going on?"

"I just got a call." I relay what happened and plop down on a chair in my living room.

"And you hung up?"

"Hell, yes, I did. I don't want to know what she wants, Maeve. It's been two years, and damn it, I'm moving on with my life. I don't want to go back there."

"Don't you think you should at least hear what she has to say?"

"No. I don't. Anyway, I need advice, and it has nothing to do with my philandering late husband."

"Okay, shoot."

"I'm going out with Cameron tonight, and I need outfit advice. He said it's not fancy."

"Okay, then I'd go with jeans and a cute top with a jacket or a wrap. Oh, wear those sexy brown boots you bought on sale. They're perfect for fall."

"But...do I like, tuck my jeans into the boots or wear the boots over the jeans?"

"They're ankle boots."

I pull the phone away to stare at it, then press it back to my ear. "The question stands."

"Your jeans will probably fall over the boots. And that'll be cute, too."

"Okay." I take a deep breath. "I'm nervous."

Maeve laughs in my ear. "Don't be. Have fun. You know Cam, so there's no need to worry that you've been catfished, that he's still married, or anything else."

"Well, that's a good point. Okay, I'd better get in the shower. He'll be here in about thirty."

"Thirty *minutes?*" she asks, clearly horrified. "Mags, you should be doing your makeup right now."

"He said it's not fancy!" I hate wearing makeup. I'm not the girly girl that my sister and sisters-in-law are. "Why do I need makeup?"

Maeve sighs heavily. "At least wear some mascara

and a little nude lip gloss. You're lucky that you have such wonderful skin so you can do the bare minimum and look great."

"Fine. Anything else?"

"Have fun. Call me tomorrow."

"Okay. Thanks. Bye."

I hang up and walk through the house to my master suite, stripping on my way there. If I have to put on a little makeup, I'd best get a move on.

I stow away my recording tools, which means that I shove it all in the closet and get busy taking the fastest shower on record, then quickly dress, changing my shirt not once, not twice, but *thrice*, and then get to work on my hair and makeup.

The doorbell rings just as I return to the living room.

The look on Cam's face when I open the door is totally worth the time I spent with the makeup and blow-dryer.

His blue eyes travel up and down my body, and when he pins me with his gaze, my knees go weak.

"Holy shit, you're gorgeous," he breathes. My breath catches, and before I can step back, he cups my face in his hands and brushes his lips over mine in the sweetest, most tender kiss I've ever had.

"Whoa."

He grins against me. "Yeah. Whoa. We should probably go catch the ferry."

I blink, trying to make sense of the words, but my

head is still spinning from the potency that is *Cam*.

"Mags?"

"Yeah? Oh, right. The ferry."

I grab my bag and sling it across my body, then wrap myself in my jacket and follow Cameron to his car.

He's in jeans that mold perfectly to his ass. His button-down is a shade of blue barely lighter than his eyes, and he's wearing the black leather jacket that's always made my girl parts sit up and take notice.

Cameron is a deliciously handsome man.

He opens the door for me and presses his hand to my back, guiding me into the car. I love how he touches me. As if it's the most natural thing in the world—as easy as breathing.

Joey *never* touched me. By the time he died, we hadn't had sex in over a year. And that was fine by me because whenever he did want to get laid, he'd just do it. No foreplay. No *fun*.

I mean, what's the damn point?

And that's the last time I'll compare Cam to Joey. They're not the same men, not at all.

And that's just one of the reasons why I'm here.

"So, what are we doing in Seattle this evening?" I ask as he pulls away from my house.

"Dinner and a show," he replies.

"What show?"

His smile is sly as he breezes through the gears on the standard transmission. "You'll see."

~

"I COULD EAT a million of these shrimp." I chew the one currently in my mouth and look around the restaurant that Cam brought me to. We can see Puget Sound from our table, but he hasn't taken his eyes off me. And not in a creepy way. It's a sexy, I-want-to-devour-you-whole kind of way.

Did I mention that it's sexy?

"I have to admit," I continue, "this might be the *easiest* date I've ever been on."

"What do you mean?" He grins and takes another bite of his steak.

"I already know you, so we don't have to waste time with ridiculous small talk. We can just *talk*, you know?"

He nods thoughtfully. "I agree. Also, I get to look at you, and that is a good time."

I wrinkle my nose at him. "Don't be cheesy."

"I'm being honest. I like looking at you."

I pop another shrimp into my mouth, not at all self-conscious about eating in front of Cameron. My phone rings in my purse, and I frown as I fish for the device, then silence it and put it away.

"Must not be important?"

I force a smile. "No. Probably someone trying to sell me a car warranty."

His eyes narrow, and he leans closer to me. "Don't fucking lie to me, Mary Margaret."

I narrow my eyes back at him. "It's honestly not important. No emergencies, and it's not the family."

He sits back, and I take a sip of water.

I'll be damned if I let some bimbo my former husband banged and had a kid with ruin my time with Cameron. She doesn't matter. She's not a part of my life.

"Do you want me to order you more shrimp?" he asks, changing the subject.

"No, I'm probably eighty percent crustacean as it is. No more for me."

"How about dessert, then?"

"That's another matter entirely." I laugh as the waitress returns to take our empty plates away and leaves us with the dessert menu. "Wanna split some cheesecake?"

"You expect me to *share* cheesecake?"

"Okay, let's get two desserts and share them so we each get a whole. How about that?"

"Better." He orders us the cheesecake and some hot apple crisp with ice cream.

I'm going to weigh fifteen pounds more when I leave here than when I walked in, and I'm perfectly okay with that. I'm enjoying him, the view, and the food.

"I'm dying to know which show we're going to see."

"*Wicked*," he replies.

"Holy shit, you got us tickets? That show's been sold out for months."

"I know a guy." He shrugs and makes me laugh. "I remember you said a few years ago that it's your favorite, but you've never seen it."

"I haven't, but the music is incredible. This is awesome, thank you."

"Don't thank me yet. We might be in the nosebleed seats."

"I don't care," I reply honestly. "Hell, we could be backstage, and I'd be grateful."

He smiles, and the server brings our desserts.

"Cheesecake and *Wicked*. You're spoiling me."

"That's the goal," he says around a bite of apple crisp.

"I HONESTLY DIDN'T THINK anyone could do as well as Kristin Chenoweth and Idina Menzel, but those women were *amazing*," I say as Cam stops his car in front of my house. It's past midnight, and we caught the last ferry of the day to the island after the show, which is still sending shock waves through me.

He smiles and then gets out of the car to open my door for me, offering his hand to help me out of the low-sitting car before walking me to the door.

"Did you like it? Or did you just tolerate it for me? Because I've been talking non-stop since we left the theater, and you haven't said much."

When we reach my door, Cam sighs and braces a

hand on the frame, caging me in. "Who can get a word in edgewise? You're like a kid on Christmas morning, and I'm not complaining. I'm glad you enjoyed yourself."

"But did *you* enjoy yourself?" I bite my lip and let my gaze fall to his mouth. God, I want him to kiss me more than I want my next breath. All through the show, he held my hand or rested his on my leg. We've been in constant contact for more than six hours, and damn it, I want his mouth on me.

"I had the best night of my life." He leans in, and I hold my breath. "And that's not a lie. It's the damn truth."

He kisses my jawline, then drags his nose over my cheek before laying his soft lips over mine in that sweet way he has.

Then, he pulls away and turns to start down the steps of my porch.

My mind reels. I don't want him to go. But then his words from the other day come back to me, and I smile.

"Are you going to come in or what?"

He pauses on the third step down, then turns back to me.

"I know it's late," I continue, "but you could come in for a drink or something."

He slowly climbs those few steps and walks toward me. "Yeah, I'd like to come in."

"Okay." I unlock the door and let us inside, flipping

on a light. "Get comfy, if you want. Since it's so late, would you rather have wine or tea?"

"Tea," he replies.

"Awesome. Be right back."

I hurry into the kitchen and fill a kettle full of water, setting it on the stove to boil. Then, I rush to my bedroom and quickly change out of my jeans and boots. Are they cute? Yes. Are they also incredibly uncomfortable? Hell, yes.

"Where the hell did you go?"

I turn just as I pull on some gray sweatpants and see Cam coming around the corner and into my bedroom. At some point, he stripped out of his jacket, untucked his shirt, and rolled up the sleeves.

I have to swallow hard.

"I had to get out of those jeans."

His blue eyes smolder, all fire and heat as they flicker down to my sweatpants. "Better?"

"Yeah. Sorry, the water should be about ready for that tea."

"After you."

I brush against him, totally on purpose, as I walk by and hear him curse under his breath. With my back to him, I let a satisfied smile spread over my lips. I like knowing that he's as attracted to me as I am to him. That he *wants* me. And, yes, in the past, that was as annoying as it was satisfying. But damn it, I'm so tired of fighting him. Of fighting *myself.* I want him. I enjoy him.

I punished us both for two damn years. I think that's long enough.

I pull two mugs down, drop a tea bag in each, and turn to get the kettle, but Cameron already has it and pours the hot water into the mugs.

"Thanks." I watch his hands and the muscles that flex in his forearms as he returns the kettle to a cold burner. A vivid memory from that night years ago flashes through my brain, sending an electric jolt through me.

His hands running over my body, caressing my breasts. Dear Jesus, he has amazing hands.

"Shall we?" He raises a brow and points to the living room. I nod.

"Yeah." I clear my throat. "Let's go get comfy."

I can't sit next to him. I'll just jump him, and damn it, this is a date, not a one-night stand. So, I curl my legs under me in the chair across from the couch where he sits and sips his tea.

He's been here before. He even spent the night once after a customer gave me a right hook to the face, and Cam stayed to make sure that I was okay. But he's never been here like this. When I know that I'd take my clothes off if he told me to.

We're crossing a new line.

"Either you need to calm down or strip out of those clothes. Because the sexual tension is so thick in this room, I could cut it with a knife."

I stare at him in surprise, and then I tip back my

head and laugh. Can he read my mind? Maybe. But the situation is suddenly so funny to me, I can't hold in the laughter. I'm being silly. I'm no virgin. And this is *Cameron Cox.*

He's right. I need to chill the hell out.

"I didn't realize I was being funny," he says at last.

"*I'm* being ridiculous," I reply and reach for a tissue so I can wipe the tears from my eyes. "Okay, I'm okay. Whew. Sorry."

"Are you *really* okay?"

"Yes." I chuckle and sip my tea. "How do you like your new house?"

"It's great. I had to replace the A/C unit two weeks after I moved in, but otherwise, it's a good place."

"Is it an old house? I think Maeve mentioned that it was built in the last century. And yes, that makes me sound old, but Maeve is the expert, and she says stuff like that all the time."

He chuckles and nods. "Yeah, in the 1960s. So things are bound to need fixing or replacing."

"Are you handy in that area?"

He sips his tea. "Yes."

"Oh, good. I'm not handy, but this house is relatively new, so I haven't had much to repair. Is your house haunted?"

He blinks in surprise, then slowly shakes his head. "No, I don't think so. Do you believe in that shit?"

"I'm Irish. Of course, I do. My old house, the one Joey bought, was haunted. Not with Joey because I'm pretty sure he's burning in hell, but with something or someone else."

"How do you know?"

"I saw her." I shrug. "You know, I realize that although you've been in my life for as long as I can remember, I don't know a lot about you."

"What would you like to know? I'll answer anything I can."

"Well, I know that work is off-limits."

He raises a brow.

"Yeah, yeah. Okay, do you have siblings?"

"No."

"Do you see your parents often?"

He sets his mug aside. "Also, no. My parents are pretty shitty. Mom left when I was small, ran off to marry some guy she'd been having an affair with. My dad still lives around here somewhere."

"Like, *here* here? On the island?"

"Yeah. He's an alcoholic and wasn't really a good role model for me. I don't like to think about what might have happened if I hadn't met Kane. Your family has been *my* family since I was in junior high. Tom and Fiona showed me what it is to be good parents, and your dad had many a serious talk with me whenever I screwed up. He paid attention, and they loved me."

"I'm so glad that you had that in your life, Cam. And I'm sorry that your parents are shitty. But it's their loss."

"Is it?"

"Pfft, yeah. I mean, you're great. You have a fantastic career and good friends. You have a good *life*. And they're missing it. But they don't deserve to be a part of it, you know?"

"Yeah, I know." He watches me for a moment. "You're really far away."

"Yep."

"Why is that?"

"Because if I sit over there, I might make a fool of myself. I'm safer over here."

He licks his lips. "What might you do, if you were over here?"

"I don't think I have to spell that out for you, Mr. Cox."

He laughs, and then to my utter surprise, stands up and rounds the ottoman that separates us, picks me up, and returns to the couch to settle me in his lap.

"There."

"Okay, I admit, this is pretty comfortable." I lay my head on his shoulder and loop my arm over his chest. Yawning, I settle in against him. "I could sleep here."

"Why don't you go ahead and do that?" He kisses my forehead. "Go to sleep, sweetheart."

"Your legs will go to sleep, too." But I yawn once more and feel myself drifting. "If I get too heavy, just move me."

"Stop worrying so much." He kisses me again. His voice rough with fatigue, he says, "Trust me, everything is just fine."

CHAPTER 4

~CAMERON~

*S*he wasn't wrong. At around two in the morning, I had to move us to the bedroom because my legs were, indeed, asleep. But she was resting so peacefully, I didn't want to wake her. After we settled on the bed, she curled around me, laid her head on my shoulder again, and never even realized that we'd moved.

I hadn't lied when I told her that I'd had the best night of my life. Nothing beats spending time with Maggie. Making her laugh, having a conversation, and watching her eyes light up as she watched the show was an absolute delight.

When I'm with her, everything in me settles as if she's my safe place. And after being in a lot of sticky situations all over the globe during my time in the Army and even part of my civilian job, it's the best feeling in the world to be here with her.

It's all I've wanted for what feels like years, and I'm finally here.

It's a good thing I'm a patient man.

Maggie sighs and then turns away from me, snuggling down into her pillow.

The girl can *sleep.* I check the time and just about swallow my tongue.

It's eight in the damn morning.

I don't remember the last time I slept this late. But we were up well past midnight, and despite having a gorgeous woman draped over me, I didn't sleep well. I just wanted to enjoy her. God knows if she'll have a change of heart later, and I never end up here again.

That would be my damn luck.

I move up behind her and kiss the back of her head. Maggie sighs again and then whispers, "Time is it?"

"Eight."

"Early."

I laugh and kiss her again. "That's pretty late for me."

Maggie wiggles onto her back, rests her hand on my arm where it lays across her belly, and blinks up at me with sleepy eyes. "I usually work until almost three, so I sleep until around eleven. My internal clock is just set that way."

"Makes sense." I kiss her forehead. "Go back to sleep."

"No, it's okay." She sighs and then frowns. "How did we end up on the bed? Didn't I fall asleep in your lap?"

"I carried you in here."

"You *carried* me?" She grins and then laughs. "Like, in a romance novel?"

"I didn't want to wake you."

"Hmm. Well, I'm awake now." Her green eyes flicker down to my lips and then back up to mine. "How did you sleep?"

I don't answer her. Instead, I lean in and kiss her. I like to tease her lips, brush them softly and elicit light moans from her throat. Her hand drifts up my arm and then dives into my hair as I sink into her, consumed by her sweet sleepiness and soft skin. And when she presses her hips against me and loops a leg over mine, I know there's no turning back.

"Cam," she whispers when I push her onto her back and bury my face in her neck. Fuck me, I love the sound of my name on her lips. The way she grips me as if she's searching for a lifeline.

But just as I slip my hand under her shirt, the doorbell rings.

"You have *got* to be kidding me," Maggie growls and pushes her hand through her hair. "If I ignore it, and it's one of my siblings, they'll just come inside to look for me."

I quickly kiss her and then pull away. "You'd better find out who it is, then."

"I'm going to disown them," she mutters as she pushes her hair out of her face and stomps across the room. "After I slash all their tires."

As she leaves the room, my phone pings with a text.

It seems this morning won't be the first time I make love to Mary Margaret.

Kane: *Good morning. I could use some help in my barn. Do you have a few extra minutes?*

I'm shocked that he's using his cell. Kane's notorious for ignoring all technology for weeks at a time.

Me: *I can be there in about thirty.*

Kane: *Great, thanks.*

I hear voices as I put my shoes on, and when I walk into the kitchen, Maeve is stirring a mug of coffee and turns her green gaze to me. She raises an eyebrow.

"Good morning." I smile at her, then kiss Maggie's temple as I brush by her to pour some coffee. "How's it going, Maeve?"

"Uh, good. Fine. Good." I glance up and see her mouthing, *"Did you sleep with him?"* to Maggie and grin.

"No, you interrupted that."

Maeve flushes, and Maggie laughs as I take my first sip of coffee.

"How's Hunter?" I ask.

"He's fine. He and Rachel went for a run on the beach, so I thought I'd come over here for a bit. But if you're busy, I can go."

"It's okay." I reach out and squeeze Maggie's hand. "Kane texted and asked if I could come help him in his barn for a few, so I'll head over there."

"I guess this turned into a busy day," Maggie replies

and takes my mug from my hand, sipping. "I work tonight."

"I'll drop in and see you. Have some dinner."

She passes the mug back to me. I drain it and then set it in the sink.

Before I leave the room, I tug Maggie to me and kiss her sweet lips. "Have a good day."

"Yeah, you, too."

I wink at Maeve, who grins like a Cheshire cat, and then show myself out.

I'd say that was a damn successful first date.

"YOU WANT ME TO *MOVE* THAT?" I stare at Kane as if he just suggested I make one of the glass pieces he's renowned for.

"I'll help," he says calmly. "It's not as heavy as it looks. You take that side. I just want it over by the wall there."

"Why are we moving it at all?"

"Because I got a new one. It's being delivered tomorrow."

"Why can't they haul the old one away when they deliver the new one?"

Kane scowls at me. "Are you going to whine like a baby or help me?"

"Fine." We squat by what looks like a big black bowl, and with some grunting and pure stubborn will, we manage to get it moved over to the place Kane speci-fied. "You're a fucking liar. That thing is heavy as fuck."

"If I'd told you that, you wouldn't have helped me." He wipes some sweat off his brow and throws me a bottle of water. "Let's go into town and get lunch. You look like shit."

"I didn't get much sleep," I admit.

"Didn't you take Maggie out last night?"

"I did."

Kane's eyes narrow menacingly. "I don't want to know about your sexcapades with my wee sister, mate."

I laugh and follow Kane out of the barn. "Trust me, it's not because of that. Come on, you can buy me a BLT at the diner in exchange for moving that heavy bastard."

"Done."

We walk straight to the car and, a few minutes later, pull up in front of the diner. It's too early for the lunch crowd, so we're escorted to a table right away.

"How did the date go?" Kane asks after we order our food.

"It was great. We had fun."

I sit back and don't elaborate, and Kane doesn't ask more.

"Good."

"How's work been going?" I ask him. "Do you have any big shows coming up? Besides at the museum."

Kane has an entire museum in Seattle dedicated to him and his glass art, and his work is on display all over the world. Royalty and presidents proudly display his pieces.

I'm damn proud of him.

"I've been asked to do a show in New York and London early next year," he says and rubs his hand over his mouth. "But with a new baby and everything else going on with the family, I haven't decided if I'll do it."

"You have literally an army of people here to help," I remind him. "Stasia won't be alone with the baby. In fact, I'm quite sure that your mother—or hers—would come and stay with her if need be. Or you can take them with you."

"It's a lot of work," he admits softly. "They want fifty-six new pieces for the show, all done by March. I'm not a glass factory, and I have a new exhibit that we're putting together at the museum. That's almost a hundred pieces in the next six months. It's not possible if I want to keep my sanity and enjoy my family."

"That sounds like a shit ton," I agree with a nod. "Tell them that it'll be a small exhibit for New York and London. Fifteen pieces, and that's it. Jesus, you're the artist here, Kane. You should have creative control of this stuff."

"You're right," he replies. "Anastasia said the same thing. I don't know why I suddenly feel like I need to please everyone. I've never been like that before."

"You always said that when the glassblowing wasn't fun anymore, you'd stop doing it."

"I'll never stop," he says, his voice hard. "It's in my blood. Part of my DNA. I'll die while making glass."

"Just like I'll likely die at a computer." We pause while the server delivers our food, and I break off a piece of bacon, popping it into my mouth. "But you don't always have to do it for a living. Christ, you have more money than you can possibly spend."

"I don't do it for the money, you know that."

"I know it. That's why I'm saying that. Don't let anyone bully you into a certain number of pieces. The museum is your baby, and it's important to you and your family. Your legacy. Fulfill that obligation first and then work on other exhibits if you want."

"That is exactly what I need to do," he agrees. "Stasia's been craving a trip to the coast. We haven't been down there since before the baby was born, so maybe we just need a few days away."

"You live on the water, and you're planning to vacation at the coast?"

"We like it," he says with a shrug. "If I thought we could get away for longer, we'd escape to Ireland."

"Now *that* I understand."

I've only been to Galway, Ireland a few times with the O'Callaghan family, but it's safe to say it's as close to heaven as I've ever been, with the greenest hills I've ever seen, and that coastline alive with temper. I could spend weeks there and not see everything.

"You should spend more time there," Kane suggests. "It's a lovely place to recharge, and that's the truth of it."

"I have work, and everyone is here. But the next time we all go over as a family, I might take extra time to explore a bit."

"Good idea. I heard from the private investigator."

My gaze whips up and finds Kane watching me. "And?"

"He didn't have much more information than before," my friend replies. "It was a quarterly check-in."

After Maggie's husband died, and the family discovered all of Joey's secrets, Kane hired an investigator. He's turned up very little information that Maggie and the others didn't already know.

Because there's nothing to find unless you're a government operative.

I know *everything.* Every detail.

And I'm not allowed to say a word to the people I love the most.

It's been the worst torture of my life.

"HERE'S YOUR STEW, some bread, and save some room for dessert." Maggie winks as she sets my food in front of me. "I made some cobbler. No, it's not Irish, but it sounded good today."

"You can go ahead and save me some."

She smiles brightly and then loads her tray with the drinks Keegan set out for her before setting off to deliver orders to her tables.

I've been doing this for years, coming into the pub to have a beer and some dinner—and watch Maggie as she weaves and shimmies through the tables and stops to sing with the band. There's nothing like Mary Margaret's voice filling the room.

I chat with the other regulars and enjoy banter with Maggie's siblings.

But it's Maggie that keeps me coming in so often. Always has been.

She lights up a room.

I notice a table of college-aged kids in the corner booth, laughing and joking with Maggie as she takes their orders. She asks for their IDs. Everyone must pass muster because she doesn't throw anyone out.

When she returns to the bar to place her order, Keegan leans over to talk to her.

"They look a little rowdy over there."

"Loud but harmless," Maggie confirms. "I'll keep them in line. But there's another table there in the middle."

She jerks her head in the general direction but doesn't point so she doesn't get too much attention from other customers.

"The one with the redhead?" I ask her.

"Yes, that one. She came in here alone and ordered a soda and dinner. That guy sitting with her just plopped himself down. I don't think she's comfortable with it."

"She's smiling," Keegan points out.

"It's forced," I reply, watching the couple in question. The dude puts his hand on her arm, and she pulls away, then says something and walks up to the bar between Maggie and me.

"Excuse me," she says to Keegan, and the man from the table walks up right behind her, listening. She frowns. "May I please have an angel shot?"

"You got it, lass." Keegan smiles and winks at her. "I've got you covered."

"She needs a beer," the asshole announces. "Not a shot."

"I'm talking with the lady," Keegan replies, then looks at the woman. "Do you want extra lime with that, lass?"

"Yes. Yes, please."

Keegan nods and then meets my eyes. Maggie immediately walks into the kitchen to fetch Shawn, and I glance up as Hunter joins us, as well.

Operation angel shot has begun.

"Sir, I'm going to ask you to leave the lady alone," Keegan says.

"What the hell are you talking about?" he retorts angrily. "I'm her date."

She shakes her head slightly, and I pat her shoulder with reassurance.

"Let's go outside for some fresh air," Hunter suggests as Shawn joins us. "You're pretty drunk, man. You need to clear your head."

"Fuck that. This is a bar, isn't it? I'm here to drink

and take this honey home for some fun, if you know what I'm saying."

Before she can reply, I grab one arm, and Hunter grabs the other as Shawn walks ahead of us to get the door. The asshole flails about, and when we toss him onto the sidewalk, he jumps up and punches me in the gut.

I see red, then come up with my elbow and clip him in the jaw, pinning him against the wall before getting in his face.

"She said *no*, asshole," I growl at him. "Now, you can leave on your own, or we can call the cops."

"Fuck you. What do you care about that stupid cunt? Give me ten minutes with her, and she won't be saying no for long."

"Motherfucker," Hunter says, pacing behind me. "Call them."

"Already on it," I hear Shawn say.

"I bet we'll find date rape drugs in your pocket, won't we?"

"Fuck you," he says again as sirens wail in the distance. "Jesus, what the hell? We were just having some fun."

"No. You weren't."

Within minutes, the cops arrive. After talking with the woman and us and finding the drugs I suspected were there, they arrest the asshole and haul him away.

"How did she know about the angel shot?" I ask as I sit on my stool once more. Not everyone knows that if they ask the bartender for an *angel shot*, it's code for *a jerk is harassing me, and I don't feel safe.*

"Maggie had the flier printed and hung in the bathroom," Keegan says. "We've had one too many girls getting harassed by drunk pricks who don't know how to take no for an answer."

"I hate guys like that," Maggie says with a scowl and then turns her head when she hears the rowdy college crowd let out some hoots and cheers. "I'll take those kids over that any day."

She leaves to check on the table in question, and I turn back to Keegan as Hunter sits next to me. "I don't like how often we have issues in here."

"It's part of running an establishment that serves alcohol," he says reasonably. "And it doesn't happen nearly as often as it does in the city. Most people just want a pint or two, some food for their bellies, and then they're on their way."

But I remember the night that Maggie got punched in the face, and it makes my stomach harden with ice.

Hunter sips his beer and glances over at me. "We love our girls, and we don't want them working where they might get hurt."

"Yeah." I take a drink of my brew. "That about sums it up."

"Maeve was attacked in one of the homes she was showing," he says. "It's not always just because of the pub or the alcohol. People just suck, Cam. But we'll do everything we can to make sure they're safe."

I turn and watch Maggie and Maeve hop up onto the stage to sing. Their pretty voices fill the air in perfect harmony.

"You've got that right."

My gaze flickers over to the redhead who'd ordered the angel shot. She's finished eating and is watching the sisters sing.

I know who she is. I know exactly who she is. But I can't tell Maggie or any of the others about her. All I can do is keep my eye on her.

I'll be damned if she'll hurt anyone I love.

CHAPTER 5

~MAGGIE~

I finish singing and stop the video recording, then take a deep breath.

It's been a good afternoon for bagging content for my social media. I just have to record one more song, and then I'll have everything I need to edit and schedule a whole week's worth of posts.

With a rigorous work schedule, I like to have things done in advance so all I have to do is publish the videos on the dates and times I want them to go live.

I've got it down to a science.

"Okay, one more song, and then we're done for this week." I take a sip of my lemon water, roll my shoulders, and reach out to press record when my doorbell rings.

"Damn. So close!" I wrinkle my nose and consider not answering. All of my siblings are at the pub tonight, and I'm not expecting anyone.

But then curiosity gets the best of me, and I close the bathroom door behind me as I rush to the front door and pull it open.

"Hey."

And just like that, my mouth waters. Standing before me in all his sexy glory is Cameron Cox. He raises an eyebrow, but I take my time and let my gaze wander all over him.

"Well, hi there."

"I brought dinner." He holds up a bag, and I sniff the air. "I just have to pop the lasagna in the oven for thirty minutes."

"Is there garlic bread?"

"I'm not a monster, Mags. Of course, there is."

"Then you may enter." I gesture for him to come inside and make a mental note that I'll have to sing that last song tomorrow before I go to work. "You didn't have to bring dinner."

"It's your night off," he says simply. "You shouldn't have to cook on your day off."

I blink at him and then watch as he unloads the bag. There's another paper bag full of crusty bread and a disposable pan that Cam slips into my oven before setting the temperature to heat it up.

"I have to use your restroom," he announces and walks out of the kitchen. He's halfway down the hall when it occurs to me that he's headed for the master. I run after him, slipping in front of him before he can open the closed door.

"Not this one." I swallow hard, short of breath. "You can use the guest bath."

He narrows his eyes. "What's wrong with this one?"

"It's uh—" I search my brain, frantically looking for an excuse to keep him out of this bathroom. "I'm having it remodeled."

"No, you're not."

"It's a mess. I haven't cleaned in a month."

He doesn't flinch. He gently wraps his hand around my throat and jawline and leans in, pressing his lips to my ear. "I'm going in this bathroom, Mary Margaret."

My core tightens—I've never been so turned on in my life. Before I can reply, he turns the knob and opens the door behind me. I close my eyes and lean my forehead on Cam's chest.

But he says nothing.

I open one eye and look up at him.

"The camera is pointed toward the shower," is all he says.

"Yeah."

"Please tell me you're not letting people watch you take a shower for money because I'll have to hunt every single one of them down and kill them."

I feel my lips twitch, so I press them together. A giggle bubbles up in my chest.

"Ew, no."

He doesn't say anything else, just waits.

"So, you're welcome to use the guest room," I say lamely.

"Are you going to tell me what this is?"

Well, damn. I glance back at my setup with the lighting and candles and my phone still held in the slot for the optimum angle and sigh.

"I sing songs for social media, and the shower has the best acoustics."

He glances down at me, then back up at my stuff, and grins. "Cool. You have a beautiful voice. Why is this a secret?"

"It's not a *secret*." I shrug a shoulder. "I just don't talk about it because it's something I do just for me. It's kind of my therapy, which I know sounds weird, but—"

He kisses my forehead. "It doesn't sound weird. Were you in the middle of this when I arrived?"

"I was about to sing my last song for the week."

"Well, go ahead and sing it. I have to finish getting dinner ready anyway."

I blink up at him in surprise. "Really?"

"Sure. Do what you need to do, Mags. I interrupted *your* evening, not the other way around."

"It shouldn't take me longer than about five minutes."

"Hey, take your time. I'll be in the kitchen. After I use the guest bathroom."

And with that, he kisses me softly and then wanders away. I watch his backside in those jeans and bite my lip.

The man has been right under my nose all this time.

A considerate, caring, sexy man. And what did I do? I was sarcastic and a pain in the ass.

"I'm an idiot," I mutter as I walk back into the bathroom, shut the door, and get myself situated once again. Just like I said, it only takes me about five minutes to record the final song for the week, and then I blow out the candles and tuck everything away in my closet until next time.

I'll edit the videos tomorrow and then get them scheduled. That's the part that takes the longest anyway.

I can smell the lasagna as I return to the kitchen and see Cameron sitting at my kitchen island, reading something on his phone.

"Thanks, I got it all taken care of."

He locks his phone and sets it aside, giving me his undivided attention. He doesn't ignore me or make me feel like his phone is more important than what I have to say.

A girl could get used to this kind of treatment.

"Tell me more about this. Not because I'm being nosy, but because I really want to know. If you love it so much, I want to know about it."

"I've always loved to sing," I remind him as I check on the lasagna. It's just starting to get bubbly. God, I love cheese. "Damn, that smells good. I'm hungrier than I thought."

He's quiet while I wander around the kitchen, gathering my thoughts.

"On a whim, about a year ago, I posted a video of me singing, and it caught on. Went *viral*, as they say. And it just sort of evolved from there. Now, I try to post something every day, or every other day at the very least. I record everything in advance to make it easy."

"How many followers do you have?"

"Just over three million."

He's stunned silent, and then he clears his throat and says, "I'm sorry, I thought you just said three million."

I laugh and nod. "Yeah, I did. It's a lot of people. Of course, thanks to algorithms and stuff, not all of those people see every post. But a lot do, and they say nice things. I ignore the trolls."

"What's your handle?"

I bite my lip. "I haven't even told my family that I'm doing this."

Cam frowns. "Why not?"

"Well, Kane wouldn't know how to use the phone to see it anyway, but I just, I don't know. I've kept it to myself. I'm not embarrassed or anything. It just feels silly."

"Why?"

"Because they all have such important things going on. Kane with his glass, Keegan and the pub. Shawn writes *movies*, and Maeve sells houses. And I'm not saying that working at the pub is dumb or anything, but I wanted something that felt like I was successful in some small way."

"And you don't think they'd be proud of you?" Cam shakes his head. "You're wrong. Hell, they'd probably arrange for you to record an album or something."

I take a long, deep breath as butterflies fill my stomach.

"You have connections through Anastasia's family," Cam reminds me. "Hell, why not call Leo Nash? The man's a rock star."

"I'm not going to use my family connections," I reply softly. "The truth is, I don't want to record an album. I like my life just as it is. But I would *love* to record just one song. In a studio, with a producer. Just once so I could see what it's like. I'm a simple girl. I don't need fame or even a recording career. I like having fun with it. I sing old Irish songs, and sometimes, I take requests. I recorded a Taylor Swift song in the style of an Irish ballad today."

I take my phone out of my pocket and bring up my account, passing it to Cameron.

"Here, you can look through while I dish up dinner. Do you have social media?"

"No. It's not secure enough. I have too much information that can't ever be compromised."

The kitchen is quiet except for the sound of me singing as he watches the videos, and I get dinner ready. Even after I set a plate in front of him, he continues viewing as he eats.

It's awkward to eat and watch him watching me. But it also feels good when he smiles down at the screen or when his blue eyes shine in what I now know is lust.

His face is so expressive.

Finally, he passes the phone back and smiles over at me. "You're fucking amazing."

I bark out a laugh and cut a piece of my lasagna. "They're just little one-minute songs, Cam. It's not a Grammy or anything. Although, it is fun when people duet and add harmony. I've even had people add instruments. Musicians are so clever."

"You're clever."

"And you're flirting with me."

"At last, she notices." He winks and watches me as he chews his last bite. "Do you have plans this evening?"

"I think I'll be hanging out with you."

He nods, taking his plate to the sink for a rinse before loading the dishwasher.

"You brought dinner," I say as I finish my food. "I'll clean up."

"If we clean together, it'll be done faster."

"Are you for real? Like, are you like this all the time or just now while we're flirting and stuff? After a few months, are you going to get comfortable and relax, and I'll find out that you really are an inconsiderate jerk who doesn't do much to help me or do nice things?"

"Breathe." He sets the covered lasagna aside to cool. "You really overthink, don't you?"

"No. Well, yes, I do, but not about this. Because it happens a lot. And it's not because someone is a jerk, actually, but because they get comfortable, and it's just not important to continue to try to impress the other person anymore."

"Okay, first of all, yes, there is always going to be some of that. It just happens, Mags. But I'm this person. I'll bring—or make—dinner, and I'll happily clean it up. I'm not going to change from Dr. Jekyll to Mr. Hyde. That's not me. That might be people from your *past*, but it's not me."

"Okay."

I turn to wipe the counter down, but I feel his eyes on my back.

"That's it?" he says quietly. He's closer now, his hands gliding over my hips. "Just *okay*?"

"Yes. What you said makes sense."

He pulls me back against him, my back to his chest, and his arms wrap around me from behind.

"I'm not anyone else you've ever been with before," he says. "I'm not those morons you've been dating, and I'm certainly not Joey Lemon."

"I know." I turn and wrap my arms around his neck. "I know that. I do. I guess that, sometimes, I need to be reassured of it. And I know that sounds dramatic or silly—"

"Whatever you need to feel secure and confident is not silly. And maybe only a little bit dramatic."

I smile and reach up to kiss his chin.

"Thank you for dinner."

"You're welcome."

He pulls me closer, cages me in against the countertop, and lowers his head to my cheek. After playfully nipping at my ear, he kisses my jawline.

And when I sigh and press against him, Cam groans and takes my mouth with his, seeming to just sink right into me. My knees fail me, but he catches me, plants the palms of his hands on my ass, and lifts me as if I weigh no more than a child.

"Bedroom," I whisper against his lips.

"You're sure?"

"Bedroom, Cameron."

He chuckles and sets off down the hallway. "Yes, ma'am, whatever you say."

After he lays me back on the bed, he wastes no time getting us both out of our clothes. I'd tell him to turn out the light, but then I wouldn't be able to see him. And *holy mother of God!*

"What's wrong?" he asks, his breath coming fast.

"Nothing."

"You look…concerned."

I meet his eyes with mine and then crook my finger. "I'm just admiring the view. You have serious muscles for a computer geek, Cam."

"You know, being in shape and working with computers isn't mutually exclusive."

I don't have time to react before he crawls over me and kisses each of my hands in turn, then places them over my head.

"Grab on to the headboard."

I don't argue as I close my fists over the iron bars of the headboard above me.

"Good girl." He nips at my lips. "No matter what happens, don't let go, okay?"

"Are you going to do something scary?"

"No." He licks a circle around my nipple. "Not at all. This is all about pleasure. Just don't let go."

"Okay. I won't let go."

I sigh when his hands roam down my torso, over my ribs, and up to cup my breasts as he feasts on them —gently at first and then with a little more force. Not to where it hurts, but just enough to make my hips shimmy and my legs move as I try to relieve the sudden pressure between them.

It's just like it was before when I was with Cam. Before he stopped and left.

Don't think about that. Just enjoy.

He's a magician. That's the only way to explain how it feels as if he's touching me everywhere at once, making my body come to life under him.

I push my hand into his hair, and he suddenly boosts himself over me, kisses the offending hand, and presses it around the bars once more.

"Don't. Let. Go."

I swallow hard. "Right. Oops."

He doesn't smile. His eyes narrow, but he kisses me and then moves down once more to continue the exploration and absolute sensual torture of before. He shoulders his way between my legs, and when his tongue swipes up and over my folds to my clit, my back arches off the bed.

"Holy hell."

"Don't let go," he reminds me with a stern voice before devouring me with his mouth. Soft licks, gentle nips. He lifts my hips off the mattress so he can open me wider and do things that are probably illegal in some states. I thrash and moan and feel the pressure building as my legs begin to shake around Cam's ears.

I couldn't let go of the headboard if I wanted to. I have to grab on to it like it's an anchor and ride the building waves of pleasure until they pull me down and drown me in the foreign sensations overwhelming me.

"Cam!" Is that my voice shrieking?

"Yes, baby, yes. Good girl." He replaces his face with his hand, and I can't hold back, I push against him, feeling wave after wave crash over me as I come apart.

I moan when he pulls his fingers out of me, and with a sigh, I whisper, "So that's what all the fuss is about."

Cam's gaze darts to mine. "What did you say?"

I lick my lips and then laugh. "Nothing."

He kisses my chest, my neck, and urges me to let go

of the headboard, then kisses each hand. "What did you say?"

"I said, so that's what all the fuss is about."

"Honey, you were married. You're no virgin."

"That doesn't mean I've ever had an orgasm."

CHAPTER 6

~MAGGIE~

*C*ameron's jaw drops as he stares down at me.

"Never?"

I slowly shake my head from side to side, keeping my gaze locked on his.

"And two years ago, just as you were about to, I answered the motherfucking phone. No wonder you were so pissed off. Jesus, Maggie, you should have told me."

Normally, I would scoff. Or be sarcastic.

But I can see from the gutted look on his face that he feels awful. So, I cup his cheeks and smile gently.

"If you do that again, I'll forgive you."

He turns and presses a kiss to the palm of my hand.

"I don't deserve to be here."

"Okay, now *you're* being a little dramatic."

He tips his forehead to mine, and with one of my hands clasped in his and cradled between us, he nudges between my legs and effortlessly slides right inside, filling me completely.

I gasp.

He groans and then looks at me with wide eyes.

"No condom."

I grin and kiss his nose. "I've got it covered."

I've been on the pill since I was fifteen.

He sighs in relief and begins to move. Slowly and with long strokes, then he picks up the pace as if he just can't help himself. As if going slower might kill him dead, right here on the spot.

He pushes up so he can look down to see where we're joined, and I reach down and press my fingers to my clit, sending more electricity up my spine and through my limbs.

"Fucking hell," he growls. "That's the sexiest thing I've ever seen in my life."

I close my eyes, tip my head back, and ride the more-intense wave of sensation. But Cam wraps his hand around my neck and says, "Eyes on me."

His blue eyes shine intensely with pure, unadulterated lust and affection. Between that and the incredible sensations moving through me, I can't hold back. I fall apart, splitting into a million pieces as I come even harder than before.

I didn't even know that was possible.

With his gaze locked on mine, Cam winces and then curses as he pulses against me and jerks as every muscle in his stellar body contracts.

It's the most amazing thing I've ever seen.

And when he's done, he buries his face in my neck and rolls to the side, holding me tightly, our bodies still connected.

"Wow," I whisper.

"Damn right."

"I HAVE TO GO."

Cameron glances up at me over his mug and raises a brow. "Okay."

"I mean, I don't mean to kick you out, but—"

"But you're kicking me out."

I shrug a shoulder. "You can stay if you want. I have a girls' day brunch with all of the sisters at Maeve's house. Since most of us work in the evenings, it's hard to get together for girls' night out, so we do girls' brunch in. Maeve's hosting today."

"Fun. Are you going to drink a bunch of mimosas and talk about the guys?"

"No. We prefer bloody Marys."

Cam laughs, and I lean over to kiss him.

"I'll see you later," he says. "I need to get home and get to work myself, actually."

"Do you have a busy day full of espionage?"

"Something like that." I grab my purse, and he follows me to the door. Before I can open it, he pins me to it, my front against the wood, and grabs my throat and jawline from behind. "I want you to think of me all day. I want you to think about me being inside of you and making you crazy."

"Already planned on it."

He chuckles. "Good girl."

And with that, he pats my ass, and we're on our way. I wave at him from my car and then blow out a frustrated breath when it won't start.

Cam waits, but after three tries, it's a lost cause. I step out of the vehicle, and he rolls his passenger window down.

"I'll give you a ride," he offers.

"Thanks. I know one of the others can give me a lift back later."

"If not, just call me," he says as I buckle my seat belt.

He doesn't say anything bad about my car, which surprises me. My siblings are always giving me a hard time, insisting that I need a new one.

But I don't want to spend money on that.

Within about ten minutes, Cam pulls into Maeve's driveway. She lives in a spectacular house on the cliffs with an amazing view of the ocean.

"Thanks again." I offer him a quick kiss and then bounce out of the car. "Have a good day, dear."

He grins and blows me a little kiss, then backs out of the driveway, headed for home. Based on the number of cars already here, it looks like I'm late.

I walk in the back door by the kitchen and grin

when I see all four of my sisters, whether by blood or marriage, sitting around, laughing and talking.

"Was that Cam who dropped you off?" Lexi asks.

"Yeah, my car wouldn't start." I hang my bag on a coat rack by the door and then offer everyone a hug. "So, he gave me a lift. He stayed the night last night."

Silence descends on the room, and then everyone starts asking questions at once.

"Did you sleep with him?" Izzy wants to know.

"I thought you hated him," Stasia says.

"It's about damn time," Maeve cheers.

"Tell us everything," Lexi puts in. "Here's a bloody Mary. We're not putting too much liquor in them because we all have to work today."

"I don't get any in mine," Maeve says with a pout but then rubs her belly and grins.

"Okay, spill it," Izzy says as I sit on a stool at the huge island and take a sip of my drink.

"We had sex."

Every single one of them grins.

"And?" Stasia asks, leaning closer. "Did you...you know?"

"Did she what?" Lexi asks.

"Have an orgasm," I answer and sip my drink again. "And the answer to that question is *hell yes.*"

"Wait, you've never had an orgasm?" Lexi demands. "What the fuck?"

"Right?" Stasia agrees. "Poor girl needs to get some of that sexual tension out."

"How was it?" Izzy asks.

"Well, I don't have any orgasms to compare it to, but it was damn good." I laugh and reach for a slice of bacon. "He's really intense in bed. Cam's so laid-back and calm most of the time, so I was a little surprised by *how* intense he was. And you'd think, after being with someone so *horrible* for so long, I wouldn't like it that Cam's bossy and grabs my throat and calls me a *good girl*. But here I am, eating that shit up."

Stasia chokes on her drink, and the others sputter and start laughing.

"Holy shit, Mags," Maeve says. "Warn a girl before saying something like that. I haven't renewed my CPR certification."

"It's true! And he, like, made me hold on to the headboard. And I got in *trouble*—the good kind—if I let go. It was freaking *hot*."

"Good stuff, isn't it?" Lexi says with a knowing smile, and I gape at her.

"Are you telling me that my brother is—?"

"A Dominant?" she finishes. "He wouldn't say so, but he has particular tastes, that's for sure."

"It's always the quiet ones," Maeve says as she pours syrup on her waffle. "I know you used to hate it when we called Joey *The Lemon*, but he so *was*, Maggie."

"Oh, he was a lemon in every way," I instantly agree. "In bed, he was just a robot, you know? I was lucky if it lasted thirty seconds. And as a husband, well, we all know that he was a piece of shit. I mean, I don't want to speak ill of the dead or anything."

We all look at each other and then dissolve into laughter again.

"Who am I kidding? Hell, yes, I do. Dead or alive, he deserves it. Because it's true. So, now I know what all the fuss is about. I'm on the downslope to thirty, and I never had an orgasm before last night. That's just...sick."

"You were an abused wife," Lexi says simply. "With a man who didn't value you in any way. It makes sense that you didn't enjoy the sex with him."

"I mean, he never hit me."

"Stop right there," Izzy says, surprising me. "I hate the whole *he-never-hit-me* excuse. He was mean to you. He said horrible things, and I've heard that he even controlled what you ate. That's abusive. When you had sex, what would he have done if you'd said no?"

All eyes turn to me.

"He got mean if I said no, so I ended up doing it just to shut him up."

"So, he was a rapist," Lexi says. "Yeah, he was a lemon."

"You went from The Lemon to The Cock," Stasia says with a big grin. "Because, you know, Cam's last name is Cox."

"Oh, that's much better," Izzy agrees and gives Stasia a high-five. "In our sacred girls-only space, Cameron will now be known as The Cock."

I giggle and take another sip, then dish up a plate. I'm starving. And I love these girls, my sisters, who make me feel good about myself and make me laugh.

"To amazing sex," Lexi announces, holding up her glass in a toast. "And to the hot-as-fuck men who make it damn fun."

"Hear, hear," Izzy says as we all clink glasses. "Also, I have an announcement."

"What is it? You're not pregnant again so soon, are you?" I say with a laugh, but then her smile turns coy, and we all gasp.

"Izzy," Maeve says. "You'd better not have alcohol in that glass."

"I don't," she says with a laugh. "It's *so* soon, I know, but it seems that I'm a fertile Myrtle, and Keegan wants lots of babies. So, here we are."

"That's fabulous," Stasia says and hugs Izzy. "I love that the family has so many new babies."

"Ma and Da will be beside themselves," I agree. "Look at us, being adults and everything."

Stasia smiles softly. "I also have an announcement."

"If you tell us you're pregnant, too, we're going to have to put the alcohol away," I reply.

"No, I'm not. But I'm shutting down my cake shop in Bellevue. With the baby and everything, it's a pain in the ass to commute back and forth. So, I'm going to start a bakery here, on the island."

"Oh, that'll be awesome," I say. "We don't have one, and we need it. I bet you could sell pastries to the diner, as well, for people who want a quick bite on the run."

"There are so many ideas," Stasia agrees. "I'll need to hire some people because I travel quite a lot with Kane, but we'll get it sorted out."

We turn to Lexi, who widens her eyes. "What?"

"Any announcements?"

"Hell, no. I'm not having babies. I'm writing a book. That's about it."

"No babies, ever?" I ask her.

"I don't think so," she replies quietly. "Shawn and I have talked about it, and for now, we're not planning on it. But we love being the cool aunt and uncle."

"You're good at it," I agree. I know that there's a big age gap between Lexi and my brother, and I wonder if that's why they're not going to have children. But it's none of my business. They're both very happy together, and that's all that matters.

"So, babies and orgasms and new businesses," Maeve says. "I'd say that's a damn good day."

"Hear, hear!"

CHAPTER 7

~CAMERON~

I've been up for hours, plugging away in my office. It's been a couple of days since I stayed with Maggie. Since we shared the best damn night of my life.

She's been working her ass off at night, and I do the same during the day, so we've been hit and miss with seeing each other aside from a few minutes at the pub. But I'll see her later. Maggie's parents are coming in from Ireland today.

I'm the only one who knows. They wanted to surprise all of their kids with a visit. So, I'll pick them up from the airport in a few hours and take them to the pub.

I know they'll be jet-lagged, and they should go to Maeve's and settle into the little guest apartment above the garage, but they'll want to go to the pub first.

Because I'll be gone for most of the day, I had to get

ahead with work this morning, and I'm just about all caught up.

Next, I have to call a major superstar. Arguably, the most famous rock star on the planet.

I can't believe I have Leo Nash's phone number, but I do, and I want to talk to him about Maggie and her incredible voice.

When I dial his number, it goes to voicemail.

Anastasia warned me that this might happen, so she also gave me his wife's phone number.

Sam answers on the second ring.

"Hello?"

"Hi, Sam, this is Cameron Cox. I'm a good friend of Kane's."

"Of course. Hi, Cam. How's it going?"

"Everything is good here, thanks for asking. Hey, I'm trying to reach Leo. I have some questions for him. You aren't by any chance with him, are you?"

"No, actually. He's at the studio in the city today, working on a new album. You're welcome to call him there. If he's recording, you can leave a message, and he'll call you right back."

She rattles off the number to the studio for me, and I commit it to memory.

"Thank you. I really appreciate it."

"Anytime. How are all the girls doing? We haven't done one of our epic girls' nights in way too long."

"Everyone is doing very well, as far as I know."

"Well, I'll be calling Nat and Jules, and we'll put

together a party soon. Thanks for reminding me that we need to do that."

I laugh and shake my head. "You ladies and your girls' events crack me up."

"Hey, we all work hard. We deserve some time to eat and drink and gossip. It's what I live for. Go ahead and call the studio. Leo will be there all day."

"Thanks again, Sam. See you soon."

We hang up, and I dial the number for the studio. A woman answers immediately.

"Hi, I'd like to speak with Leo, please. This is a friend calling. Cameron Cox."

"Sorry, we don't have anyone here by that name."

She hangs up, and I stare at the phone with a frown. For fuck's sake.

I call back, and she answers again.

"I believe we were disconnected. I'm a friend of Leo's, and I'd like to speak with him, please."

She doesn't even reply, simply hangs up.

I run my hand through my hair, swear under my breath, and then decide to go to the city early. I have to go over and pick up the parents anyway, so I'll go an hour before I planned to and swing by the studio on my way.

I text Maggie and let her know that I'll be off the island for a few hours and then set off toward the ferry.

I'll handle this in person.

∽

IT'S A CLEAR, pretty spring day in Seattle, so the ferry ride is uneventful and arrives on time. I drive through town to the studio, which sits just across the street from Nic Montgomery's bakery. I'll have to go in and get some cupcakes on my way to the airport.

After miraculously finding parking at the curb, I toss some coins into the meter and walk into the studio, surprised to find Leo standing at the counter.

"Cam! Hey, man, what's up?"

He crosses to me and does the man handshake-hug combination, with a genuine smile on his face.

"I tried to reach you earlier, but your receptionist hung up on me."

Leo raises a brow, and then we both look at the woman seated behind the counter. "What the hell, Judy?"

"Do you know how many people call here asking for you? If I put every call through, you'd yell at me for letting fans interrupt you."

"I did mention that I'm a friend," I reply.

"They all do," she says, rolling her eyes.

"Next time," Leo says, not unkindly but firmly, "take a message, and I'll call back the ones I want to."

"Yes, sir," she says and reaches for the ringing phone. "Sorry, no, he's not available, but can I take a message?"

She rolls her eyes again, and Leo just smirks and gestures for me to follow him. "Judy's been here a long time and thinks she's irreplaceable. And she's probably right. But that's no excuse. Sorry about that."

"It's fine, I had to come this way anyway. I feel weird about this, but I have a favor to ask."

Leo leans against a desk and crosses his tattooed arms over his chest. "Shoot."

"You know Maggie O'Callaghan."

"Sure."

I go on to tell him about her social media account, the millions of people she has following her, and Leo tugs his phone out of his pocket and pulls her up while we're talking.

Maggie's voice fills the air.

"Damn," he whispers. "She's good."

"I know. Now, she says she's not interested in recording an album or seeking a career as a pop star, but she'd love to professionally record *one* song."

Leo tucks his phone away and looks over my shoulder as if he's formulating a plan.

"You know, I'm in the middle of recording a new album. There's a song on it, a ballad, that would be fabulous for her if she'd like to sing it with me."

I grin at him, and Leo smiles back.

"Let's make a plan."

"YOU'VE ALWAYS BEEN SUCH a good lad," Fiona O'Callaghan says from my passenger seat and reaches over to pat my arm. I drove my truck today because it has the extra room, with four doors and cargo space. The Mustang wouldn't work for airport runs.

"I'm just glad you two were able to come," I reply and glance back at Tom, who's watching the island pass us by as I drive us over to the pub. "Everyone is going to be so surprised."

"You're the only one of our children who can keep a bleeding secret, and that's the truth of it," Tom says with a laugh.

Every time these amazing people call me one of their kids, my chest swells. I don't know how I got so lucky to be brought into this fold, but I'm grateful for it every damn day.

I pull up to the pub, and we all get out of the truck. I take charge of the luggage as Fiona makes a beeline for the door.

"It's excited she is to see her wee babes," Tom says, that Irish lilt as thick as ever.

"And they'll be excited to see her," I agree. Tom rolls one of the suitcases, and I take the other. "How long do you think you'll be in town?"

"Until after Maeve has the baby."

"That's a few months away, at least."

"It is, aye. Fiona wants to be with her girl for the bulk of the pregnancy. There's nothing quite like having your ma nearby, is there?"

I wouldn't know. But I can say that there's nothing like having Tom and Fiona here.

Before I can answer him, Kane calls, and I answer on speaker.

"What's up?"

"Hey, are you back on the island?"

"How did you know I wasn't on the island?"

"Maggie told me."

"Yes, I'm back."

"Great, can you please come over to my place? There's a situation, and Maggie's having a bit of a fit."

"I am *not* having a fit, you arse," I hear Maggie yell in the background.

Tom snorts next to me.

"Sure, I can come over. Give me about fifteen, okay?"

"Thanks."

Kane hangs up, and I blow out a breath. "Well, looks like I'll say hi to everyone and then head over to Kane's."

"It wouldn't be a lovely Wednesday if Maggie wasn't worked up about something," Tom says with a laugh. "She's a spitfire, that one is."

"You're right about that, Tom."

I rest my hand on the other man's shoulder before we go and find the others.

"Yes, lad?"

"I need to talk to you about Maggie."

He firms his lips but doesn't say anything, waiting for me to continue.

"I'm dating her."

His eyes light with humor, and he smacks me on the shoulder. "It's about time, my boy."

"You're okay with it?"

"Is there a reason I should forbid it?"

I shake my head and rub my hand over my mouth. "No, sir. But I'm older than she is by about a decade, and some might find that disturbing."

Tom's quiet as we listen to Keegan and Izzy exclaiming and fussing over Fiona. They're obviously surprised and excited.

"I've known you the majority of your young life," Tom says at last. "And I couldn't love you more as a son than if you'd been born from Fiona's body. You're part of our family."

"And I'm grateful."

He turns to me in surprise. "Grateful? It's not gratitude that any of us want from you, boy. We just want your love and respect."

"And you have it, in spades."

"I know we do." He calms and pats my shoulder. "Maggie didn't grow up with you the way the others did because she was so much younger, so it makes sense that it's not a brother she sees when she looks at you. It's a good man you are, and any father would count himself lucky to know that you have your eyes on his daughter."

"Thank you." Relief brushes away the heaviness I've carried on my shoulders.

"She's been hurt before," he continues. "And I trust that history won't repeat itself."

"No." I shake my head. "I'd rather die than ever hurt her. I love her."

"Have you told her that news yet?"

I grin and shrug one shoulder. "Not yet. I don't think she's ready to hear it. But we'll get there. There's no hurry."

"You're a smart man," Tom says and claps me on the back as we walk toward the kitchen. "A smart, smart man. I think you got that from me."

"I think you're right."

"Da!" Keegan exclaims and hurries over to hug his father. "How did you keep this a secret?"

"We had Cameron help us," Fiona says. "Now, that's a lad who can keep a secret. If we'd told anyone else, it wouldn't have been a secret at all."

"I'm offended," Shawn decides. "I can keep a bloody secret."

"Right." Lexi rolls her eyes and then laughs. "You're a vault."

"I am," Shawn insists but then chuckles. "I don't care who kept the secret. It was a damn good one. I'm so glad you're here."

"As are we, boy," Tom says. "Now, is there some stew simmering? This old man needs something in his belly."

"You ate on the plane," Fiona reminds him.

I slink away to go put out a fire at Kane's place. I

don't know what he's done this time to rile Maggie up, but she sounded good and pissed on the phone.

Exactly nine minutes later, I walk into Kane's house and through to the sunporch where we usually sit when we're here. Kane has a killer view of the ocean.

Murphy, Kane's yellow dog, runs over to greet me, and I scratch his ears.

But I narrow my eyes when I see the other two people in the room.

Maggie.

And Bill Miller, the private investigator that Kane hired after Joey died.

"Why is he here?"

"Wait." Maggie rounds on me, fire shooting from her magnificent green eyes. "You know about him? You *know?*"

"Okay, let's calm down," Kane says.

"Fuck that," Maggie says. "I told you that I was done. I don't want to know any more about the shit that Joey pulled. It's over. I'm moving on with my damn life, so anything that he has to say is irrelevant to me."

I stare at my best friend incredulously, then sigh and push my fingers into my eyes to try to relieve the headache that's set up residence just behind them.

"I wouldn't have asked you to come here if I didn't think the information that Bill has is valuable," Kane says. "And before you cut my bleeding head off again, you'll shut up and listen, Mary Margaret."

If looks could kill, Kane would be in a bloody heap on the floor.

"I don't mean to upset you," Bill says. "There hasn't been much to find that you didn't already know. Until about two days ago."

He opens his briefcase and pulls out some paper copies of documents and photos.

"I stumbled upon this account and safety deposit box belonging to a Lemonade, LLC in the Cayman Islands."

It's about time you found that account, you idiot.

Maggie's eyes widen, but then she shrugs. "So?"

I want to pull her to me and tell her that everything will be okay. But when it comes to this matter, I don't know how much reassurance or support she wants from me. She's been hell-bent on healing privately, almost from the minute she found out that her husband was dead.

"So, your safety deposit box key probably goes to that," Kane says.

"I don't care," she insists. "I don't freaking care, Kane."

"That's bullshite," Kane replies, his voice raised in frustration and his Irish accent stronger. "You have an opportunity to find out what's in that damn box."

"And the account is worth half a million dollars," Bill adds.

"I'm probably not the beneficiary," Maggie says. "He had a dozen accounts, and I wasn't the beneficiary on any of them. Not to mention, it's likely money he stole, so it doesn't belong to me anyway."

"That's why he stashed it down there," Bill says, echoing my thoughts. "It can't be traced. *And*, you are, in fact, the beneficiary."

Her mouth opens and then closes again.

"Bullshit."

"Not bullshitting you," Bill says patiently. "All you have to do is go down there with your identification and claim it."

Maggie sits on the couch, and Murphy lays his head in her lap. She absently pets his head.

"Half a million," she whispers. So many emotions cross her face all at once—going from confused to sad to angry once more.

"I don't want it."

"Mary Margaret," Kane begins, but she cuts him off.

"I don't want it," she repeats and digs into her purse, coming up with the key before throwing it at her brother. "If you're dying to know what's in the box, *you* go look."

"Only the beneficiary can claim it," Bill informs her.

"Please," Maggie says with a roll of her eyes. "He has more money than God and can talk his way into just about anything. He'll figure it out."

And with that, she kisses Murphy and stomps out of the room.

Murphy whines.

Kane curses.

Bill sighs.

"You're a fucking idiot," I inform my best friend. "I told you to drop this a year ago. She doesn't want to know. She made it clear, but you wouldn't let it go."

He drags his hands down his face. He's pissed. But so am I.

"Look, I know that you want to protect her, but goddamn it, Kane, she's not a child. She doesn't want this."

And anything else that he finds can only hurt her further.

Joseph Lemon was a grade-A son of a bitch.

"She's pissed," Kane mutters.

"Yeah, at me, as well. And if you fuck this up for me, I'll never forgive you. I suggest you fix it."

I turn and stomp out of the house and out to my truck. Everything in me wants to run after Maggie. I'm pretty sure she went straight to the pub, and by now, is telling Keegan and her parents and anyone else who'll listen what just happened.

They've got her for now.

I need to figure out a way to diffuse her anger with me. Because, yes, I knew about the investigator. And, frankly, I know a hell of a lot more than that. But I can't tell her—or anyone else—what I know.

And some days, that knowledge feels like it's strangling me.

I spoke with my former boss and asked if I could tell Maggie, *just Maggie*, what I know, and he adamantly said no. This matter falls under the jurisdiction of the US government, and I'm legally bound to keep quiet. If I don't, I could go to jail for up to ten years.

I'm not willing to do that.

Not today or any day.

Besides, Maggie insists that she doesn't want to know, so it's been no harm, no foul.

Until today.

I don't think I can mend this with a bouquet of posies and some chocolates. She's too angry.

Instead, I swing through the dollar store and buy a dozen drinking glasses, then I pull up to my house and haul an extra tin trash can from my garage and put it in the bed of my truck before driving over to Maggie's.

I don't have a key to her house, but that's okay. For what I have in mind, I don't need to go inside.

CHAPTER 8

~MAGGIE~

*G*oddamn it.

Goddamn it!

I should go straight home so I can stomp around and scream in frustration, then go to the pub once I've calmed down a bit.

That's what I *should* do.

But that's not what I'm going to do because I need to vent, and I need someone to validate my feelings.

I'm just so *pissed off.* I want to punch someone. I want to break things. How dare Kane and Cameron go behind my back and hire an investigator after I specifically told them not to?

It's not their decision to make!

I come to a screeching stop at the pub and march inside, seeing red.

But I come up short when I see my parents sitting at the bar.

I blink, rubbing my eyes.

"Am I hallucinating?"

"There's my wee lass," Da says, and just like that, all of the anger leaves me, and I start to cry.

I didn't realize how badly I needed to see my parents until just this second.

"Well, what's the matter?" Ma croons as she hurries over to me and pulls me in for a hug. "There there, darlin'. It can't be that bad now."

I can't reply. I can only cling to her and cry into her shoulder. She leads me to one of the booths, and Ma and I get cozy, snuggled up together. She strokes my hair and whispers soothing words until my sobs subside into soft whimpers.

"I never cry like this," I manage.

"That might be why you needed it," she replies and wipes my face with a napkin. "There, now, tell me what has you in such a state."

"I'm mad."

"About what, exactly?"

"Your eldest son is a pain in my ass, that's what."

Her hand pauses in my hair and then keeps moving again. "And what did Kane do?"

Why do I feel like I'm five again and tattling on my brother?

I sit up and reach for more napkins to wipe at my face and blow my nose. "You know I did my best to move on after Joey died. After everything that I learned about him, and how horrible he was. And just when I thought that everything had calmed down, and I was through the worst of it, something happens to smack me right in the face. It's like he's dead, but he just won't *die*, you know?"

Ma narrows her eyes and nods slowly, continuing to brush her fingers through my long, red hair.

"What did the no-good bastard do now?"

"Which one, Kane or Joey?"

Her lips twitch. "Either one."

"Kane called me this morning and asked if I could come over for coffee. The jerk made it sound as if we could just enjoy a quiet morning together. And we don't do that very often anymore, so I jumped at the chance. But he tricked me."

Ma raises her eyebrows. "It's a trick, is it?"

"There was another man there. A private investigator. Apparently, Kane hired the guy shortly after Joey died to uncover all the things we weren't finding on our own. Even though I told him *not* to do that. And the guy said that he found an account in the Caymans that Joey owned, and I'm the beneficiary."

"How much money is it?"

"Half a million."

If she were wearing pearls, she'd be clutching them in her pretty hands. "Mary Margaret."

"There's a safety deposit box, too. So the key I have probably goes to that."

"And where's the problem?"

I stare at her incredulously. "They did this against

my wishes, Ma. *And* Cameron knew! He showed up, and he already knew what was going on. I'm sleeping with him, and he betrayed me."

"You're sleeping with Cameron, are you?"

I wince. "I said that out loud, huh? It doesn't matter. I don't want any of this. I don't want the money or the box or anything else."

"Seems to me you could use the money," Ma says. "Whether you use it for yourself or donate to a cause."

The door to the pub opens, and Kane walks in.

"I don't want to talk to you."

"Too bad," he says and slides into the booth opposite us. He blinks at Ma. "How in the world did you get here?"

"By plane, just this morning. My sweet Cameron came to get us and kept our secret. And it's happy I am to see you, but I'm going to let you talk with your sister for now."

She kisses my cheek and then scoots out of the booth and joins everyone at the bar. She says something to Da, who then looks my way and gives me a wink.

"I'm really, *really* mad at you," I inform Kane. My eldest brother reaches for my hand, and I don't pull away. Of all my siblings, I'm closest to Kane, and that's saying a lot because we're all tight.

"I know, and I'm sorry that you are," he says, measuring his words. "But I'm not sorry that I hired Bill. You deserve to know everything that Joey did, and if he left some money for you, well, you're entitled to that, as well."

"But I don't want it," I repeat. "Kane, I've worked damn hard to leave that part of my life behind, and you keep cutting me off at the knees every single time you undermine me like this. I know that you think you're doing what's best, but only *I* know what's best for me. I'm not a little girl anymore."

"I just want you to consider going down to the islands to check it out. If you don't want the money, donate it," he insists, echoing Ma's thoughts, "but don't let it just sit down there, making that bank richer. It might bring you some closure."

I take a deep breath. "I don't want to talk about this anymore. You're not hearing me. I'm going to go home, clean up, and rest before work tonight. Just give me some space, okay?"

"Mary Margaret, I love you. You know that."

"I know it. But, sometimes, you love me too hard."

I get out of the booth. Before I leave, I lean over to kiss Kane's cheek. I may be mad at him, but I love the big jerk.

I also swing over and give my da a big hug and then assure Keegan that I'll be back for the start of my shift.

I need a shower and something to eat. I have some leftover stew in my fridge that will do because I'm not going in to work early to order something from the kitchen.

I'm looking forward to a long, hot soak in the

shower when I turn onto my street, but then I scowl when I see Cameron's truck parked at my curb, and the man himself sitting on my steps.

I park and get out of the car, propping my hands on my hips as I approach him.

"I don't have time for you right now." My voice is harder than intended, but that's okay. I'm mad at this jerk, too. "You'll have to come back another day."

"I'll settle for this day," he retorts and stands. "And I have something for you in the backyard."

"Look, I'm not ready for you to try to suck up to me. I just want to take a shower and eat something so I can clear my head for work later. I'm mad at you and Kane and Joey all over again, and it's damn exhausting, Cam."

"I know."

"And if I dwell on it, I'll want to hit something, and it's just best if you go home."

"I know that, too. But I'm not going home. Come on."

He takes my hand and leads me around the house, through the gate, and into my backyard.

"Why are the men in my life so damn hell-bent on making me do shit I don't want to do?"

"You're going to want to do this. Here, wear these." He passes me some clear safety glasses, then points to a garbage can set up on the patio and a box next to it. "There are two-dozen cheap glasses in that box. How about you smash them?"

I frown up at him. "Do you need a doctor?"

"I'm serious. Here, I'll go first." He walks over, chooses a glass, and smashes it into the garbage can, making it shatter. "Feels damn good when you're frustrated."

I join him, choose a glass, and let it fall into the can.

"That was pathetic. You have to smash it like you mean it. Like you're aiming for Joey's face."

He presses a new glass into my hand, and I rear back, then throw it down with all my might.

"You son of a bitch, Joey."

The glass shatters, and I have to admit, it *did* feel really good.

"See?" he says with a grin. "The whole box is for you. Go for it. Destroy it. Be mad."

I reach for another, and then another. I cuss out Joey and Kane and Cameron and break glass, and it's possibly the best therapy I've had in a long time.

When I'm done, my chest heaves, my muscles sing, and Cam's grinning at me like a loon.

"Better?" he asks.

"A little, yeah. That was better than flowers and chocolate."

"I have chocolate on the porch," he says and cautiously reaches for my hand. "I was covering all my bases."

"Why didn't you tell me about this Bill guy?"

He sighs and brushes a lock of my hair off my cheek. "Over the past couple of years, you haven't really wanted to have conversations with me. Mostly, you snapped at me."

I close my eyes and rest my forehead on his chest. "Yeah, well, you could have told me."

"Sure, I can see it now. *Hey, Mags. Go to hell, Cam. Sure, but by the way, we hired a PI to look into your asshole of a late husband. Okay, great, thanks.*"

I laugh and then playfully push him away. "Whatever, smartass. Where's my chocolate?"

"I'm hoping you'll share."

"Not a chance."

I DON'T KNOW why the pub was so busy on a Sunday night, but we were *hopping* all day. I haven't bustled about so much since tourist season.

My feet aren't used to it. I need a hot shower and some tea before I fall face-first into bed for a good, solid eight hours.

I wave at Keegan, who always comes outside with us girls when we leave so he can watch us get into our cars safely. It's not a bad neighborhood—there are no bad areas on the island—but you never know what might happen outside of a bar after closing time. Keegan waits until I start my car because it's been iffy lately, but on the third try, it turns over. My brother waves back, and I pull out of the small parking lot behind O'Callaghan's Pub.

I decide as I turn right that I'm glad it was a busy day. Today would have been my ninth wedding anniversary to Joey, and with everything else that's been going on lately where he's concerned, he's been invading my thoughts too much.

"God, you're stupid. Just take the car to the garage."

"I work at night and sleep during the day, so if you could make the arrangements, that would help."

"Stop being lazy."

I clear my throat and turn again.

"You're too fat. Stop eating all that junk at the pub. If you weren't fat, I might want to fuck you once in a while."

A car with bright headlights passes, and I have to squint to see. Once it's gone, my steering wheel starts to shake, and then...my car just dies.

"Fuck." I lean my forehead on the steering wheel and feel my eyes welling with tears. "You just gave up the ghost, a mile from home, at three in the freaking morning?"

Resigned to walking, I gather my jacket and purse, leave a note on the dash that I'll have it removed in the morning, and start to walk home. My already-tired feet are *not* happy.

Could I call someone? Sure. Anyone would come to get me, but I feel like I kind of deserve this. I'm the one who let the damn car limp along for a few years, even though I knew that it needed to either be replaced or go in for major work.

But who can afford that?

I can't. Not right now.

"I can walk around the island," I remind myself in the dark. "It's not that big. And if it rains, I can catch a ride. Actually, Kane has a couple of extra cars I'm sure he'll let me borrow until I can replace that one. It'll be okay."

"You're always depending on your stupid family for help. Grow up and be your own woman."

I hate having Joey in my head. I haven't heard these shitty things in a long, long time. He was the meanest at home when we were alone. If he got really mad, he'd raise a hand to me but never actually slap me. Mostly he preferred to sling words about as weapons, and he loved to intimidate me. Probably because he knew the words hurt most, and if he left marks on me, my brothers would kill him.

I can't believe I made excuses for that jerk. I brushed off their concerns and told them that everything was fine, even when it was far from that. Because I was embarrassed and because I felt stuck with Joey. Where would I go? What would I do without him? It was just easier to stay.

And then he died, and while part of me grieved, the bigger part of me was relieved.

And I felt guilty for that. That I hadn't been strong enough to just leave him. Instead, he died, and I was off the hook.

When I discovered that he'd only left me with the few thousand dollars in our checking account and nothing else, I didn't even care. Because I was free of him.

"You were an asshole, Joey," I say out loud. "I don't even have very many good memories from our marriage. Because shortly after we said *I do*, you were off doing God knows what with God knows who. And I was here, fending for myself."

I walk up the front steps to my door and take a deep breath when I'm safely inside.

I don't know, the idea of having all that money currently sitting down on that island is tempting. It would replace that bucket of rust that just gave out on me.

Considering it, I walk back to my bedroom and strip out of my clothes for that hot shower. I start the water so it can heat up and wipe the makeup off my face. I turn to step into the water and scowl.

Usually, by the time the makeup is gone, the shower is ready for me.

But there's no steam, and when I reach my hand in, it's still ice-cold.

"No." I shake my head and quickly wrap a towel around me as I run to the tiny mechanical room just off the kitchen where the hot water heater resides.

It's not making any noise.

I'm no water heater expert, but I'm pretty sure it's supposed to make noise.

"Don't do this to me," I plead, but deep down, I know it's fruitless.

It's dead.

My car is dead.

"What else?" I ask as I pad back to the bathroom. "I hate asking my family for help. I'm almost thirty, I shouldn't have to ask for help."

I decide against the shower and instead take a sponge bath. I'll need to wash my hair in the morning, but I'll do that in the sink.

At least I can wash my jeans in cold water.

I check my pockets and pull out the key that Kane gave back to me during my shift this evening.

I hold the brushed-gold-colored key up in the light.

If what that Bill guy said is true, there's enough money waiting for me that I could not only fix what needs fixing but put plenty away for future emergencies, too. I could even pay Kane back for the down payment on my house.

"After we got married, all you did was make me feel bad, Joey Lemon." I sit on the edge of the bed and stare down at the key. "You told me I was worthless and made me feel that way. You humiliated me with your many girlfriends and a *child* that wasn't mine."

I bite my lip and sigh.

"Maybe I should consider claiming the money."

"So?" Maeve passes me the maple syrup and stares at me with a bland expression.

"So, what?"

We like to get together a couple of times a month for brunch, just the two of us. One day, I go to her place, and the other day, she comes here to mine.

Rachel's out of school today, so she came with her. I love spending time with my niece.

"So, are you going to a tropical island to get rich?" Rachel asks before popping a piece of pineapple into her mouth. Maeve stares at her. "What? I heard you telling Dad about it. I'm seventeen, not deaf."

I can't help but laugh at her. I take a bite of a pancake. "I don't know. Part of me really doesn't want to."

"Look, I totally understand and agree with you not wanting to have anything to do with The Lemon."

"Me, too," Rachel adds. "He sounds like he was a huge jerk."

"But that's a lot of money, Mags. You need a new car, and you won't let any of us help you with that." Maeve continues. "You need a nest egg for a rainy day. There's nothing wrong with collecting money that a man you were married to left for you, even if he was the asshole of the century."

She's not wrong. Not to mention, no one else knows that my hot water tank died on me, and I don't have the fifteen hundred dollars to replace it.

I about swallowed my tongue when I got that estimate. And let me just say, taking cold showers isn't a delight.

I need hot water.

I need a running vehicle.

And while the pub pays me enough to pay my bills, it's not enough to get ahead. I know that Keegan would pay me more, but it's not right. I thought for so long that Joey left me with nothing but embarrassment—and in a lurch.

Maybe this would be the one good thing to come out of that shitshow of a marriage.

"Earth to Maggie," Maeve says, waving her fork in front of my face.

"Sorry. I'm thinking about going to collect the money."

Her jaw drops. Rachel grins.

"There's no use in me being a stubborn ass. Kane was not completely wrong when he said to not let the bank continue making money off what's mine."

"When are you going?" Maeve asks as Rachel carries her plate to the sink for a rinse.

"I'm not sure. I need to think about when I can get away, but probably sooner rather than later."

"Why can't I get any hot water?" Rachel asks, and I cringe.

"Don't worry about it," I reply. "You can set it in the sink, and I'll take care of it later."

"I think you should get that money as soon as possible," Maeve says, a knowing look in her eyes. "Like, yesterday, Mary Margaret."

"I just told you, I'd look into it. Don't nag."

A quick knock sounds on the door, and then Cameron walks in, stopping when he sees all of us in the kitchen.

"Am I interrupting?" he asks.

"Nah, it's just breakfast," Rachel replies. "Want a pancake?"

"If I can steal Maggie away, I don't have time for a pancake."

"Steal her," Maeve says, waving us off. "I'll put stuff away and lock up."

"Are you sure?"

"I know how to lock up," Maeve says. "Go, have fun."

I grab my purse and keys and follow Cameron out to his Mustang.

"Where are we going?" I ask once we're on the road.

"Seattle," he replies and squeezes my hand. "To Leo Nash's studio."

I turn in my seat and stare at him. "What?"

"Just trust me." He pulls my hand up to his lips. "Don't worry."

"YOU WANT me to sing with you?"

I look up from the music in my hands and stare at Leo in surprise.

"I do, yes. I've heard you sing, Maggie, and I think

your voice would sound great on that song. You'd be helping me out."

I bust up in laughter. "Right." I can't stop laughing. "I'd be helping *you* out."

Tears form in the corners of my eyes, and I wipe them away.

"I want you on the song," Leo says and shrugs his shoulders, showing off his ridiculously impressive, tattooed arms.

It's no wonder Izzy has a huge crush on him. Leo Nash is an incredible specimen of a man.

"When are we doing this?"

"Right now," Leo replies. "We're ready for you in the studio."

"*Now?*"

"We're here," Cam adds. "And we have time."

Suddenly nervous, I rub my hands on my jeans and then stand and square my shoulders.

"Okay, let's do this."

"Right on," Leo says and wraps an arm around my shoulders as he leads me down a hallway to a recording booth.

It's bigger than I expected, with a soundboard behind a big, plexiglass window. The studio has microphones and instruments, and Leo's band is already in their places.

"This is a live recording?" I ask in surprise.

"It's my favorite way to work," Leo says as he joins me in the booth. Cam is in the production room with two other men. "We're going to run through it without recording first so we can get a feel for each other and the song. If you want to tweak anything, just tell me. This is an original song, so we can do whatever we want with it."

"You wrote it?" I ask.

"Yeah, and you won't hurt my feelings if something doesn't sound right to you, and we need to work it out."

"Okay, cool. Let's do it."

For two hours, we work. The song is an absolutely beautiful slow song about a lost lover and the emptiness he feels since she's been gone.

It reminds me of an Irish ballad, and I tell him so.

"Do you want to add more wind to it?" Leo asks. "To make it even more so?"

"No, I think this rock edge is cool. But let's work on the hook a bit. I feel like it's missing a beat."

Leo nods and grabs a guitar so he can pick while we sing. In ten minutes, we have the rough patch fixed, and we return to the mics with our headphones on as the band grabs their instruments.

This time, when we start from the beginning, we nail it. I know it as soon as the last note reverberates through the room.

This is it.

This is the one.

"Hell, yes," Leo says with a wide grin and pulls me in for a hug. "This song is going to be a hit."

"It's okay if you put it on the B-side, and it's never heard from again."

Leo pulls back and frowns down at me. "First of all, this is the twenty-first century. There are no more B-sides. Second of all, this might be the first single we release from the album."

I can't move. Hell, I can't breathe.

"You're going to *release* it?"

"Why else would we record it? I'm assuming you don't have an agent, but don't worry, I won't screw you. We'll make sure you're paid a fair percentage and work out the details."

"I'm not doing this for the money," I reply immediately.

"Yeah, definitely no agent," Leo says with a laugh. "This is a job. Cam told me that it's not a job to you, but it is all the same. If you ever change your mind about wanting to make a career with your voice, just let me know. Even if you don't want to be a single recording artist, I can always use backup vocals on the road. It's something to think about."

I can't even reply.

"You should invest in some recording equipment for your house and practice. Technology is incredible these days. You can record on your own and upload it to one of the media streaming services, a website, or a bunch of other places to sell your music. Make a little money. Think about it."

"Thank you." I can't help it. I launch myself back

into his arms and hold on tight. "Thank you so much, Leo. You didn't have to do this."

"I'm glad we did," he says softly and hugs me back. "You're incredible. Isn't she, guys?"

"One of the best voices I've heard in years," Gary says with a nod. "And I'm not blowing smoke up your ass."

I laugh and wipe at a tear that I didn't know had formed. "If nothing else, this was really good for my ego."

"When we go on tour with this album, if you want to join us for this song and as backup vocals, we'll hire you in a heartbeat," Leo says.

I gape at him and then laugh.

"Okay, enough. I have plenty to think about here. Thank you so much for this. It was seriously an item on my bucket list that I can now mark off."

"I'm glad."

Cam comes into the room and scoops me up in a hug. After we listen to the song twice more, we say our goodbyes and head back for the island.

When we're at the railing on the ferry, I look over at Cam and watch the wind blowing through his hair for a minute.

"Will you take me to the Caymans?"

His blue gaze whips over to mine. "You want to go?"

"Yes. I need recording equipment. And a car. And some other things. And, damn it, I more than earned that money. I'm going to claim it."

"Good girl." He pulls me close and lowers his mouth to mine. "We can go whenever you're ready."

"I'll talk to Keegan when we get back. I'd like to go as soon as possible."

"We'll arrange it, then."

CHAPTER 9

~CAMERON~

"*H*oly shit, this is nice," Maggie says as we step inside the hotel suite. She wanders to the window and looks out at the ocean, then turns back to me with a grin. "The water looks way different here than it does back home."

"No kidding." I walk over to her and slip my arms around her waist, burying my face in her hair. "I know you're nervous, sweetheart. You don't need to be."

"I don't know why I am." She turns and wraps her arms around my middle, hugging me tightly. "It almost feels like when I go into that bank tomorrow, I'm going to find Joey standing there, and the idea of that makes my stomach hurt."

"He's not here," I reassure her and feel my chest clench. "Honey, I never asked you, and you never said, but did Joey hit you?"

I watch the clear, blue water gently lapping against

the white sand below and brace myself for Maggie's answer. I don't need or want to know everything that happened inside their marriage, but I've often wondered if he laid hands on her.

"He raised his hand to me a couple of times," she admits softly, and it takes everything in me not to tense up. "But he never actually hit me. Because he knew that if my family ever found out, they would likely kill him. And I know people use that as an expression, but you know my family." I nod, and she keeps going. "He liked to mock me, make me feel bad about myself. He controlled what I ate because he thought I was fat."

"What?" I pull back to frown down at her. "Mary Margaret, you are *not* fat. You have curves, the way a woman is supposed to. What the hell was wrong with him?"

"I know that," she insists. "I know, Cam. I'm not fat. And even if I was, who cares?"

"Exactly. And who the hell did he think he was that he could speak to *anyone* that way? What a fucker. I want to beat the shit out of him."

Maggie laughs, and her hands move up my chest and around my neck. "Easy there. Like you said, he's gone. And I know that, deep down, but I'm nervous because that money is clearly stolen, Cam. He didn't make that much of a salary as a financial advisor. What if the money really isn't mine, after all? And what if I find something awful in that damn box? I'm sick and tired of surprises from him. They're never good ones, so I guess I just don't trust this."

"I'll be there with you, and we'll deal with it as it happens. That's all we can do."

"I wish we didn't have to wait until tomorrow morning," she whispers. "I just want to get it over with."

"It's after six in the evening," I remind her and kiss her nose. I can't stop kissing this woman. "The bank is closed. But I have dinner coming up through room service, and then I thought we would take a walk on the beach."

"Well, that sounds nice."

"I thought so, too. We're both too travel-weary to go out."

"I definitely don't want to go anywhere. What's for dinner?"

A knock comes from the hall. "You'll see in just a minute."

I open the door for the room service attendant who's dressed in a black tux. He wheels in a cart, gets everything set up on the dining room table near the windows, and even sets a vase of yellow roses in the middle, then takes his leave.

"This is fancy," Maggie says, eyeing the table. "I feel underdressed."

"Personally, I think you're *over*dressed. I'd rather have you naked."

She laughs and shakes her head. "I'm not eating

naked. I don't want to spill something hot on my boobs."

"I tried." I sigh as if incredibly disappointed and make her laugh.

I uncover the plates and hold the chair out for Maggie.

"Steak?" she asks as she sits and leans over to sniff her plate. "With all of my favorite things."

"Coincidentally, they're my favorite things, too, so it works out."

I sit across from her, ready to dig into the delicious-smelling meal. I'm starving.

"I didn't even realize I was so hungry," she admits, echoing my thoughts as she cuts into her steak. "Mm, good."

She's right. The steak is tender and practically melts in my mouth. We had a long travel day full of junk food. We need *real* food and rest so we're ready to deal with whatever happens tomorrow.

And from what I know about Joey Lemon—and that's literally everything there is to know about the son of a bitch—anything could happen.

"Oh, God," Maggie moans as she tries her potatoes. "I don't know what they put in here, but I need the recipe."

"Moan like that again, and I'll have you on this table." I drink my wine and watch her blink in surprise. "I don't think you realize how much you turn me on."

"Because the food is delicious?"

"Because you're sexy as fuck."

She swallows, licks her lips, and I see those green eyes have gone smoky with desire. I want her. I *always* want her.

It never stops.

I eat my dinner, and Maggie follows suit, her eyes still on mine, the sexual tension between us so thick we could cut through it with these steak knives.

When we've both finished our meals, I take her hand and lead her to the bedroom.

"I thought we were going for a walk on the beach." But she doesn't pull away when I tug her to me and kiss the hell out of her.

"We will." I kiss her cheek. "After."

The grin that spreads over her sweet face is more intoxicating than the wine we had with our dinner, and when I nip at her lips, she lightly gasps.

"Everything you do, even when you frustrate the hell out of me, turns me on."

Maggie snort-laughs. "Yes, I'm sure I'm sexy as all get out when I'm throwing one of my tantrums."

"You have no idea." I nip at her chin. "You're so full of fire, so indignant, I want to pin you against the wall and fuck you until you don't remember your name."

The laughter leaves her, and she stares up at me with stunned green eyes. "Really?"

"Oh, absolutely." I tug her shirt over her head and let it fall to the floor, then cup her perfect breasts in my palms. "Every damn time you snapped at me, I wanted to pull your hair back and kiss you."

Maggie yanks my shirt up and over my head, our movements becoming frenzied in our need for each other.

"I don't know if I would have complained."

Her bra hits the floor.

"You would have hit me."

My jeans are open, and her hands slide down my bare backside, urging the denim down around my ankles.

"Maybe," she admits and bites my shoulder.

I get her out of her jeans and then simply rip her panties off her.

"Definitely." I pick her up and toss her onto the bed, then climb on after her. "But I don't know if I'd mind all that much."

"If I hit you?"

"Mm."

She snort-laughs again, then moans when my hand finds her core and sinks into the wetness of her folds.

"Ah, hell," she groans.

"Always so wet," I murmur against her lips. "Always ready for me."

"It's your own damn fault." She swallows hard and arches her back. "You have a habit of getting me all worked up."

"Well, darn." I grin and watch her gorgeous face as she falls over the first crest. "That's my girl. Good girl."

"Jesus, you make me lose myself." She pushes on my shoulders, and I roll onto my back, where she climbs on top of me and runs that mouth over my torso. "I could just eat you up. Why do you have to be so delicious?"

"I could ask you the same."

"I don't have these muscles," she mutters and licks my abs, almost sending me through the roof. Her hand wraps around my cock, and it's safe to say that the tables have been fully turned.

I usually like to be the one in control, but with Maggie, I don't mind at all if she wants to take the helm for a while.

She licks and sucks and makes me see stars, but before I come, she straddles me and lowers herself onto my cock.

I cup her ass.

She braces herself on my chest.

"I want to ride you," she says. God, when she's turned on, her eyes shine like emeralds. As if she's some kind of gorgeous sea witch or a siren. I just can't say no to her.

I never could.

And I never will.

Her naked body, with curves in all the right places, moves effortlessly, and when she reaches back to cup my balls, I know it's over for me.

The room spins.

The stars explode.

I come hard and fast, anchoring myself with Maggie, her hips gripped tightly in my grasp as she grinds and pushes against me, succumbing to her own climax.

"Hell, yeah," she pants and then chuckles breathlessly as she stares down at me. "The sex is just so good with you. You've ruined me for all others."

Good.

"I'm not sorry."

She grins and pulls off me, then pads into the bathroom, her naked ass moving back and forth with each step.

I've always been an ass man.

"I want ice cream," she calls out from the bathroom. I can hear water running, then it shuts off, and she walks out again, not at all shy in her nakedness. "And that walk on the beach."

"In that order?"

"In any order." She sits next to me and pushes her hand through my hair. "I feel better."

"Good." I grasp that hand in mine and kiss it. "Let's go get that ice cream and then walk on the beach with it."

"Okay." But before she leaves me to get dressed, she leans in and presses her lips to mine in a soft kiss. "But I want two scoops."

"Greedy girl."

THE ROOM IS CAST in that soft, blue-gray hue of early morning. The sun isn't up yet, but it won't be long before it makes an appearance.

I glance to my right and frown when I find the bed empty. A quick brush with my hand tells me that Maggie's been out of it for a while.

The sheets are cool.

I sit up and brush my hands over my face, then visit the restroom before taking off through the suite, looking for her.

To my dismay, she isn't here.

I prop my hands on my hips and glance out the window, seeing a single person walking on the sand.

Maggie.

I'd recognize her red hair anywhere.

I hurry to dress and make my way downstairs and through the breezeway of the resort that leads to the beach.

Maggie's about a quarter of a mile away wearing a flowy, white dress that floats in the wind. Her loose hair gets caught by the breeze, and she doesn't reach up to tame it.

She's clearly lost in thought.

By the time I reach her, she's turned to the surf and sits her cute butt in the white sand.

I sit next to her, and she reaches out for my hand, linking our fingers. We sit that way for a long time. No words, just the sound of waves and tropical birds.

After what seems like ten minutes, Maggie begins to speak.

"We've always been drawn to the sea, my family and me. It's why Da took the family from Ireland to Seattle all those years ago. Because it was in the States but reminded him of home with the rugged coastline and the moody ocean. Whenever I need to think, I find the beach. The noise drowns out all of the voices in my head, and I'm able to just *be*."

She turns to me. "Thank you for being the one to come here with me. I don't think I could have come alone."

"You're braver than you give yourself credit for, Mary Margaret." I kiss her cheek. "You can do this."

"I know." She takes a deep breath and then shrugs. "Actually, I don't know. I've been doubting myself all morning."

"If you don't want to do this, we can get back on a plane this morning and go home until you *are* ready. Or, we can wait a couple of days if you want. Take a little vacation."

"I could make excuses for the next ten years to get myself off the hook." She pushes her hair off her face. "And I'm over being scared by that jerk. I'm taking control of this, and we're going to go to that bank today. I'm claiming what's mine."

"What are you most afraid of?"

She turns back to the water and takes a long, deep breath.

"Good question. I'm not worried about the money. That's just policy stuff and red tape. It'll get figured out. But the box?" She shakes her head. "I'm afraid of what's in it. Why would he have something in a box in the Caymans? Because he was hiding something, that's why. And he hid a lot of things, Cam. I think I found most of them. None of them were good."

I squeeze her hand, unable to tell her that she's finally found the last thing.

"And I've decided that this is it. Once I close the account and take whatever's in the box, I'm closing the book on my life with Joey Lemon, for the sake of my mental health. I *need* to move on, Cam. I need to say goodbye to him for good and get on with my life. *We* deserve that."

"I agree." I press my lips to her temple and wrap my arm around her. "You deserve to make the life you want, Maggie, without the weight of what Joey was and did hanging over your head. He's dead and gone. I think it's the right move to finish this today and then put it to rest."

We're quiet again as we stare out at the water. As the sun rises, Maggie stands and holds her hand out for mine.

"I need coffee," she says and plants her feet so she can help me up. She's damn fucking adorable. "But food will wait for after. I don't want to throw up."

"Coffee, no breakfast. Check."

"I didn't realize I had walked so far down the beach. How did you find me?"

"Your hair." I lock my fingers with hers. "You don't blend, Mary Margaret."

"I never have." She shrugs and then laughs. "Blending isn't my specialty."

"Good. I like it that way."

CHAPTER 10

~MAGGIE~

This is it.

I thought the bank would be bigger. Grander. I know enough to know that people keep millions, if not billions, of dollars here to *hide* it from the feds. So, because it houses so much dough, I'd thought for sure it would be a big, important-looking building.

But it's not.

It's white and square, and if I'm being honest, it appears kind of institutional. If there weren't huge guards with guns just inside the door, you'd think it was a hospital or something.

One of the guards checks our IDs and then escorts us to one of the bankers.

"Geez, they're sticklers for safety," I whisper to Cam, who just nods stiffly.

Maybe he's more nervous than I am.

This part of the day runs pretty much the way I thought it would. We're escorted to a little office where a banker collects my identification and the death certificate I brought with me. Then, he leaves—I assume to verify my information.

"I wonder—"

But Cam cuts me off by leaning over to kiss me, then whispers in my ear, "We're being watched."

I fold my lips closed, and the nerves start to set in.

Of course, we're being watched. Why didn't I think of that? This isn't your friendly neighborhood credit union, for God's sake.

It feels like we wait forever, but when I glance at my watch, it's only been ten minutes when a different banker returns, his face in serious lines.

"I'm Mr. Santiago," he says. "I've verified that you are the beneficiary on the account in question. The death certificate is in order. How would you like the funds?"

"How much is it?"

His lips tighten.

"It's not like I've been receiving regular bank statements."

Mr. Santiago turns to the computer and taps some keys. "Seven hundred thousand, eight hundred and seventeen dollars and thirty-six cents."

I stare at him, stunned.

That's a hell of a lot more than five hundred thousand.

"If you issue me a cashier's check—"

"We should wire transfer this much money," he says, cutting me off.

"Of course." I glance at Cam, who nods and takes my hand reassuringly. "I'm sorry, I'm not thinking straight. I have my account information."

"Excellent. We will transfer the funds, and you will check with your bank to ensure the money has been received."

It takes no time at all. Before I know it, while on the phone with my bank in Washington, I'm the better part of a million dollars richer.

"Is that all?" Mr. Santiago asks.

"No." I pull the key out of my purse. "There's a safety deposit box here that I also need to collect."

He goes back to tapping those keys, then hums. "I don't see one."

"Listed under Lemonade, LLC," Cam replies.

More tapping.

"Here it is. Let me verify something." Mr. Santiago narrows his eyes, scrolls through the screen, and then nods. "Yes, here it is. You are the beneficiary. I'll show you back."

There's no paperwork from the money transfer, which feels a little weird to me, but I guess that's the whole point of this place.

No paper trail.

We're shown down a long hallway and into another small room with a table and three chairs.

"If you'll wait here, I'll go get the box."

"We'll accompany you," Cam replies. "You understand."

"Of course."

The room is *massive.* Rows and rows of boxes, that have to be twenty feet high. Mr. Santiago finds the correct box and slides a key in, then I slide my key in, and we turn them together.

The door opens and reveals a simple metal box, just like in the movies.

"You may look through the contents here, or in the room we were in before."

"I might need to sit down," I reply. "Can we please go back to the other room?"

"Of course."

He says that a lot. I briefly wonder if it's the same as when southern women say, *"Bless your heart."*

Santiago leaves the room, and Cam and I sit next to each other, the unopened box on the table.

"Are we still being watched?" I whisper.

"Undoubtedly."

I nod and open the extra bag I brought with me. "I'm just going to dump it in here, and then we can look through everything at the hotel."

"I would also prefer that," he says calmly.

I open the box and am stunned to find *another* box. So, I transfer it to the bag, and then Cameron and I stand to leave.

No one stops us as we make our way through the

bank and outside. We don't say a word as we walk the two blocks to the hotel, head up on the elevator, or even when we're in the room. We just stand and stare at each other.

"Do hidden accounts collect interest?"

"As far as I know, not much."

I nod and wonder why there was such a discrepancy between what Bill said was in there and what was *really* there but then shrug.

I don't have it in me to be a super-sleuth. Like I told Cam earlier, I'm done. The money is in my account, and now it's time to see what's in the box.

"It's not heavy," Cam points out as he sets it on the table by the windows.

"With my luck, it's empty." I bite my lip and then reconsider. "On the other hand, that would be the best-case scenario. Okay, let's get this over with."

I open the lid on the white box and frown. On top is a crisp envelope with *MAGGIE* written in block letters.

"That's his writing," I mutter and pick up the envelope, setting it aside. The only other thing inside is a black velvet box, likely from a jewelry store.

"Read that first," Cam suggests.

I pull a letter out of the envelope and begin to read aloud.

Maggie,

If you're reading this, it's because I'm dead, and you've found the account and box down here in the islands. I wonder how long it took you to find it? I think I hid it all pretty cleverly.

I'm not going to tell you where all the money came from because I don't want you to ever be held responsible as an accessory. I'll just say that it can't be traced, and now it's yours. You probably found other money in other places, but that was for Constance and Heather. I didn't think I'd ever be a father, but I am, and I have to provide for her.

Of course, there were other women. Too many to name here. Am I sorry for that? No, not really. I'm sure it hurt you, but I have needs that you couldn't deal with. Not your fault, just the way it is. Don't be too hard on yourself for it.

I roll my eyes and glance up at Cam, who looks like he wants to commit murder, then I keep reading.

I'm pretty sure that everything I've done will catch up with me and kill me. Whether it's because of the women and their husbands or other reasons. I won't live to be an old man. I can't leave this for you in a conventional account. It would be seized. This way, it can't be.

Also, the other little present in here, well, don't worry. It's not stolen. I bought it, fair and square. Just another way to hide money. It's worth about a hundred grand. Do whatever you want with it.

I know that I was a shitty husband, and you should have had better at the end of the day. But from the minute I saw you in Algebra, junior year, I wanted you for myself. And I have you. I don't know if I love you, honestly. You can be such a royal pain in my ass, and you complain constantly, but you're beautiful, and that's all that really matters. Oh, and if I am *dead, go ahead and tell your brothers to fuck right off. I hate those assholes.*

Take the money and do what you want with it. It's yours. And, yeah, I'm a shit, but I do hope you have a great life, Mags. Better than what you had with me.

J.

Cam takes the letter from my hands, skims it, then folds it and puts it back in the envelope.

"He was a prick," he says at last.

"Yeah, I don't feel so bad anymore." I blink, surprised by how light I feel. "Okay, let's see what this is."

The box is hefty, and when I push the lid open, diamonds shine in the sunlight.

"Holy shit."

Cam looks over my shoulder. "There have to be a hundred karats here."

The necklace looks like it should be on the neck of royalty. It glitters and shines when I move it from side to side.

"What in the hell am I going to do with it?"

"You don't have to decide today. Or any other day. Put it away, and deal with it later."

I nod thoughtfully. "You're right, there's no rush. Although, I'll never wear it. It's...gaudy."

I close the box and then stare over at Cam.

"It's over."

He nods slowly. "Was it worse than you thought?"

"No." I ponder the question and reach for an apple

from the bowl of fruit on the table. I'm suddenly starving. "Not harder. But not easy, either. About what I expected, actually."

"And now that it's over, how do you feel?"

"Lighter." I take a bite of the apple. "A lot lighter, actually. You know what's funny? That letter didn't hurt my feelings."

His eyebrow goes up, and he starts to protest, but I keep talking.

"I'm serious. He said so much worse to me when he was alive. I didn't really expect much more from him. I knew he didn't love me. You don't treat people you love like that. And I *wanted* to love him. But I didn't. Hell, I laughed at his funeral."

"I think that probably happened out of shock," he says kindly.

"Okay, so it took one of his mistresses yelling at me to make me laugh, but still. So, no, this didn't hurt me. And, frankly, it sounds like he's trying to be sweet in the letter. He was just such a complete, selfish asshole that this was as good as it got with him."

"I suspect you're right," he says. "Please tell me you don't feel weird about the money anymore."

"I don't." I blink, surprised at my quick response. "I really don't. He didn't tell me who he stole it from, so I can't return it. And now I can get my hot water heater fixed."

"Wait, your water heater is broken?"

"And I can replace my car. And buy some recording

equipment. But does it make you feel weird that I have more money than you?"

Both of his eyebrows go up now, and then he laughs a little. "Who says you do?"

"I...you...wait, what?"

He just laughs again and shakes his head. "We'll have to set you up with a financial planner. You can't just have that much money sitting in a checking account."

"I know. Kane has a guy."

"I have the same guy," he says, and I'm even more intrigued.

"Cam, you never told me that your job made you rich."

"You never asked."

"I—"

"I said I couldn't tell you *what* I did and what I do now. You never asked about the rest. I do okay."

"Right. You do okay. Sure."

"Why are *you* acting weird?"

"I'm not acting weird."

"Yeah, you kind of are." He reaches over and pulls me against him. "It's just money, Mags."

"That's easy to say when you have it."

He kisses my forehead. "You're right. And I haven't always had it. What I do can be dangerous, and I'm well compensated for it."

"Being a computer geek is dangerous?"

His eyes close into slits, and I grin.

"Yes."

"What could happen?"

He sighs. "Imprisonment. Death. Any combination of the two."

My heart stutters. *Death?* "You have to quit."

"Maggie—"

"You have to quit *today*. We have enough money. You don't have to do that anymore. It's too risky. Just quit."

"Hey, I'm fine." I shake my head, but he holds on tight. "Listen to me. I'm *fine*. The *really* dangerous days are behind me. That was mostly when I was in the Army. These days, everything is on the up-and-up and much less dangerous."

"Don't just tell me that to placate me, Cameron Cox. I mean it."

"It's the honest truth."

I sigh and feel a little teary. I had no tears when I was dealing with the last of the Joey stuff this morning, but the very thought of losing Cam reduces me to a blubbering mess.

"If you're lying to me, I swear to God, Cam…"

"I wouldn't lie to you, not about that."

"Okay. Wait, is that how you knew that we were being watched at the bank?"

"Anyone with two eyes could see the cameras. Well, anyone who isn't preoccupied with closing her dead husband's account, that is."

"Yeah, I was a little distracted. Do you think they could hear us, too?"

His lips twitch up into a patient grin. "Yes. Yes, they could hear us."

I nod and glance back down at the box. "Do you think you can find out who this necklace belongs to?"

"In about ten minutes. Come on, we'll order up some food and I'll start doing some digging."

"Okay."

"What do you want to eat?"

"My ma's shepherd's pie. But I'll settle for a burger."

"We'll be home by tomorrow night, and you can have all the shepherd's pie you want."

"I'm ready to go home. Wait, why can't we go today? I have a *lot* of money, Cam. I can charter a flight."

"Okay, Daddy Warbucks, there's no need for that. We can just see if we can change the flight to today."

"Oh, right. Or that."

"That money's already burning a hole in your pocket."

"No, I just want to go home. I want my family."

"I get it. Okay, let's get a flight out today, and we'll figure out the necklace later."

"I have to get on a flight with that thing. What if they arrest me? Holy shit, Cam, what if they seize it and arrest me for smuggling or theft?"

"You've watched a *lot* of movies, haven't you?"

"Hey, it could happen."

"It won't. Just pack it in your purse. Trust me."

"Oh, God, I wouldn't do well in a Cayman prison."

"I don't know. You'd probably have a good view of the ocean."

I slap his arm, and he laughs.

"You're not going to prison."

"Says the man who's not at risk of it. Maybe I should hire the plane, after all. Less questions."

"You're a bit of a drama queen. You know that, right?"

"If I booked a charter flight, we could join the mile-high club."

He laughs and then swats me on the butt. "Don't tempt me."

CHAPTER 11

~CAMERON~

"*W*ould you like something to drink?" The words are whispered so they don't wake Maggie, who's finally sleeping in the seat next to me.

I shake my head at the flight attendant and accept the offered blanket, taking it from the plastic cover to drape gently over Maggie.

By some miracle, we were able to get the last two seats in first class on a direct flight to Seattle. It'll be late by the time we get home, but we didn't care.

Maggie wanted to be home, and I can't blame her.

I've never been prouder of someone in my life as I was when she sat in that office in the bank and took care of her business. She was professional and cool as a cucumber. She was completely out of her element but held her own, asked the questions she had, and was utterly amazing.

She didn't show any nerves at all until we got back to the room.

It was fascinating to see the burden of everything Joey did lift from her strong shoulders. She was lighter. Quicker to smile.

Relieved.

And I was right there with her. I've never been so relieved for someone to have intel. Because I already knew most of what she found, and I couldn't tell her. Now, she understands what I do. There are no more secrets. No more accounts to find or secrets lurking that could spring up and hurt her.

She has all of the information.

And I can breathe a sigh of relief and be with the woman I'm completely in love with. We can build a relationship without Joey *The Lemon* hanging over our heads.

Maggie stirs next to me as we begin our descent into Seattle. She looks over at me and grins.

"We're almost home," I say and take her hand in mine.

"We still have a ferry ride," she replies with a yawn. "But that's okay. Did you sleep?"

"No." I kiss her hand. "But I'm glad you did. Did you know that you snore?"

Her green eyes widen in horror. "I do *not*."

"I would have taken a video, but I didn't want to embarrass you."

"Cameron Cox, I do *not* snore."

She glances around to make sure that no one is laughing at her, and I can't help but chuckle.

"You're not funny."

"I'm sort of funny." I kiss her hand again. "You didn't snore. Much."

"Since when are you so mean?"

"*Mean*? Me?"

She simply glares at me and then snorts and gets her area ready for landing.

"You'll be staying the night at my place," I inform her.

"I will?"

"Yes. You don't have hot water at your house, and I'm sure you'll want a hot shower."

"Oh, right. Yeah, I definitely want that. I'll call the repair guy in the morning. Hopefully, he can fit me in right away. I also need to buy a car."

"We can go into the city on your day off and find one," I offer.

"Can't I just buy one online? I don't care what vehicle I get as long as it runs."

"Well, you can, but I would think you'd want to test-drive something before you pay thousands of dollars for it."

"I suppose you're right." She scrunches her nose. "Okay, we'll go later this week."

"You really have no interest in your choice of car? No vehicle that you're dying to have?"

"Not really."

"Oh, baby, we'll have to work on that."

"I SHOULD BE TIRED," Maggie says two hours later after we walk into my house, and I set our bags inside. "And I am, but I'm not quite sleepy. Do you have any food here? I can make us grilled cheese sandwiches or something."

She opens the fridge to check out the contents.

"I totally can. You have all of the ingredients. What do you think?"

"You make it, I'll eat it."

Her face lights up in a big smile. "Fun. Middle-of-the-night grilled cheese. Do you have wine?"

"I do. Red or white?"

"Since I've never paired a wine with grilled cheese before, let's go with white."

She sets a pan on the gas stove, and armed with butter and bread, gets to work while I uncork a bottle of white wine and pour two glasses.

"People pair wine with cheese all the time," I remind her. "This is a fancy meal."

"Right." She winks and piles cheese on a sandwich. "When I was a kid, I remember getting up in the middle of the night and finding my da in the kitchen making one of these. He said he'd never heard of it until he came to the States, and it's a delight that every person should eat at least once a month."

"That sounds like him."

She smiles softly. I know she's very close to her father.

"Were you surprised that they showed up the other day?"

"I was shocked. When I found them at the pub the day that you and Kane pissed me off, I just started to cry."

"Maggie, I'm sorry—"

"No, it's okay. I mean, it's not *okay*, but I'm fine now. It was just a lot of emotion, and I fell apart for a minute. It's not a big deal. I love that they're here until after Maeve has the baby. It means they'll be here for *months*, and there's nothing better than that."

She slides a finished sandwich onto a plate, cuts it in half, *diagonally*, and passes it over to me, then gets to work making another.

I crunch into the crispy, hot grilled cheese and moan.

"Good?" she asks.

"Holy shit. I had the ingredients for *this*?"

Maggie laughs and nods. "I could have added some of that turkey you have in the deli drawer, but I wasn't sure how long it's been in there."

"Probably best you left it off," I say and take another bite. "We should make this a regular thing."

"If you like this, you should try it with my home-made tomato soup."

I stare at her and then stuff more into my mouth before I do something stupid like ask her to marry me.

We'll get there but not because she taunted me with soup.

With her sandwich done, Maggie sits on a stool and takes a bite. "Mm, good. Not as good as my da's, but it'll do."

"It'll do." I chuckle and put my plate in the dishwasher. Before I can turn around, Maggie has wrapped herself around me, her face pressed to my back, and her hands clamped together against my stomach. "Hey, you okay?"

"Yeah. I am. I'm great, actually, and I'm really grateful."

I scowl and pull her hands apart so I can turn and look at her.

"Grateful?"

"I know that Kane or my parents—or any of my family—would have gone down there with me, but I'm relieved that it was *you*. So, thanks for going with me."

"Honey, I don't think even an act of God would have kept me away. Are you going to finish that sandwich?"

She laughs and then shakes her head. "I'm done. You can have it."

Rather than reach for it, I tip her chin up. "Hey. Seriously, I'm glad I was there. I'm also glad that we're home, and you can put the hardest stuff behind you."

"Yeah." She lets out a breath. "Exactly. I think the trip and the emotion of it all is catching up with me."

"Do you want to take a shower real quick?"

"Yes, I have airplane smell on me now." She wrinkles her nose. "And germs. I'll be quick."

She kisses my chin and then hurries down the hall.

"I'm going to borrow a T-shirt," she calls out.

"Take what you need," I yell back as I finish her sandwich and add her plate to the dishwasher.

I haul the suitcases into the bedroom and quickly unpack mine, separating the laundry and taking the toiletries to the bathroom.

"Is that you?"

"I hope so." I grin at her as she peels back the shower curtain and gives me a long, slow look from head to toe.

"It's a little lonely in here."

"Is that so?" I toe off my shoes. "We don't want you to be lonely."

"And my back needs to be washed."

She disappears again, and I strip out of my clothes, then join her in the shower.

"Hi," she says with a grin. "Fancy meeting you here."

"You're in a fun mood for someone who's been awake for pretty much twenty-four hours."

"We should have more fun," she says and reaches out to grab my ass. "You have a good butt."

I pour shower gel into my hand and then get to

work washing Maggie's back. "Thanks. You have a good everything."

"Nah, I have cellulite on my ass."

I spin her around so I can examine said ass, dragging my soapy hands all over her.

"I see no evidence of this."

"You're just not looking very hard."

"No, I'm looking. Trust me, I'm looking."

She giggles. I run my hand around to her breasts and tease her nipples.

The giggle turns into a sigh.

"You're really good with your hands."

"We're a little too chatty."

"You don't want to talk with me?"

I press my lips to her ear. "I want you so worked up you can't remember what words *are.*"

"Oh."

The water sluices over us, rinsing away the water as I press Maggie's back against the tile wall.

She yelps from the cold, and then I boost her up and easily slide inside her.

"Oh, God," she moans. "I never thought shower sex was fun."

"Why not?" With one hand braced on the tile, I drag my nose up her neck.

"Because it's cold. And wet."

"Let's warm you up."

It's fast, and it's hot, and by the time Maggie's a

quivering mass of orgasmic need, the water has turned cold.

"Come on, let's get you warm."

I turn off the tap and reach for a towel, but Maggie just grins.

"I can't feel my legs. I'd say I'm fine for now."

I laugh at her, then manage to get us both dry and into bed.

"Can't keep my eyes open," she whispers.

"Go to sleep." I kiss her forehead, and with Mary Margaret wrapped around me, I drift off to sleep with her.

"I HAVE to go meet the hot water heater guy," Maggie informs me.

"I believe he's a plumber," I reply with a laugh and tuck her hair behind her ear. "I'll drive you home in just a few."

"I can walk."

"No need. I have to go see Kane this morning."

"Are you going to tell him all about what happened yesterday?"

"No, that's not my story to tell. I'm going to drink his coffee and eat his food. We get together every Friday morning for breakfast."

"I didn't know that." She pauses and looks over at me. "How long have you done that?"

"For years. If I'm in town, we have a standing date. It's been more regular since I moved into the house and don't travel for work anymore."

"That's kind of cute."

I narrow my eyes at her. "*Cute?*"

"Yeah." She grins and sashays over to pat my cheek. "You're so *cute.*"

"Men aren't cute, sweetheart."

"No?" She widens those eyes in mock surprise. "What are you, then?"

"Manly. Rugged. Handsome." I sniff and pound my chest with my fist. "Me man."

"Okay, ruggedly handsome manly man, I have to go home. I'll actually be able to do my laundry today."

"You could have brought it here."

"It's fine." She shrugs and pulls her suitcase behind her, her purse slung over her shoulder. "Ready?"

"Maggie, you really need to learn to ask for help."

"My thingy is being fixed today. I don't need help."

"Okay, stubborn girl. Let's go."

I take the suitcase from her, follow her out to my truck, load the case in the back, and we pull out of the driveway.

"Oh, do you mind if we swing by Maeve's really quick? I know it's out of the way, but I want to see my parents, and—"

"It's fine," I assure her and turn toward the cliffs where Maeve and Hunter live. Hunter's in the driveway with Tom, both men with hands on their hips, and Tom's face brightens when he sees Maggie get out of the truck.

"Well, it's a fine morning when I get to see my wee daughter." He kisses Maggie's cheek. "How are you, then?"

"Fine. Great, actually. I know that the whole family will want to hear everything that happened, but I wanted to give you and Ma a quick rundown before I meet the hot water heater guy at my place."

"Plumber," I add helpfully.

"Well, come on up then," Tom says, motioning for his daughter to go with him up to the apartment above the garage.

"I'll be right back," Maggie says to me and joins her dad.

"It went well?" Hunter asks.

"Better than expected," I say with a nod. "What are you two up to?"

"Maeve wants a garden," he says with a long-suffering sigh. "Not just a few flowerpots here and there, but entire flower *beds*. And she wants an herb garden. And a salsa garden. What the hell is a salsa garden?"

"I—"

"You know what? I don't want to know. Tom and I were just looking around, trying to decide how to arrange things."

"Shouldn't Maeve do that?"

"She doesn't want to be bothered with that part," he replies. "I'm telling you, she got pregnant, and now she has the weirdest ideas. Just out of the blue! And don't you dare tell her I said that, or I'll never hear the end of it."

"Does Maeve even like salsa?"

His jaw firms, and then he shakes his head and lets out a laugh. "I don't know. That's a good question."

"Okay, I'm ready," Maggie announces as she comes hurrying around the garage.

"That was fast."

"I filled them in really quick. I don't want to miss the ho—the plumber."

I shake Hunter's hand, and then Maggie and I are back in my truck, headed to her little house. There's no plumber truck in the drive when we get there, but there is a sedan that looks like a rental.

And on the porch, just getting ready to knock, is a woman I recognize.

"Who's that?" Maggie asks.

Fuck. Fuck, fuck, fuck.

Just when I thought there were no more secrets between us, I'm reminded that I was wrong.

And this one's a doozy.

We hop out of the truck, and Maggie hurries up to the porch.

"Can I help you? Wait. You're the woman from the pub. The one that creep was harassing."

"Uh, yeah. Right." She clears her throat. "Um...my name is Heather, and I've been trying to reach you for a while now."

Maggie takes a step back and clenches her fists.

"I want you to leave."

CHAPTER 12

I don't want this.

I do *not* want her here.

I back up until I bump against Cameron's chest, and he grips my shoulders to steady me. I can't hear over the rush of blood in my ears. My heart feels like it might pump out of my body.

This is worse than when I found out that Joey was dead.

"Easy," Cam whispers in my ear. His hands skim up and down my arms soothingly. "You're okay."

"I want her gone," I say as I shake my head in denial. After everything I've already gone through, *this* can't be happening.

"Please," Heather pleads. "I only want to talk to you. I didn't know about you until about three months ago, I swear. He lied to me, too. I only want to talk."

Heather's eyes fill with tears.

"I came from Texas. I've been trying to reach you by phone, but you always hang up on me."

"So, you just show up? Me hanging up the damn phone should have been a hint that I don't want to talk to you."

"Just give me fifteen minutes," she says. "Please?"

"Let's go inside and not give the neighbors anything to talk about," Cameron suggests, leading me toward the front door. "I'll escort her out after fifteen minutes if that's what you want."

I don't know how my numb legs carry me up the front steps. I feel disassociated from the rest of my body.

And I'm so damn angry.

Cam helps me unlock the door when my fingers tremble, and I miss the keyhole, then waits while we—Heather and I—walk into the living room and sit in opposite chairs.

I saw her the other night at the pub, but I didn't really take her in. She's pretty, with red hair and blue eyes, and she's petite. Much shorter than I am. And curvy. I can see why Joey was attracted to her.

"I don't want to hurt you or bother you," Heather begins. "I just need some answers, that's all. I didn't know that Joey was married."

I roll my eyes, and Heather shakes her head.

"I *didn't*. I met him…oh, God, eight years ago? And I'll spare you the details, but I ended up pregnant fairly quickly. Joey was thrilled. He even proposed to me. For three years, we lived together as a family, completely normal."

My hands fist in my lap, but she keeps talking. When the plumber knocks on the door, Cam excuses himself to take care of it.

What would I do without him?

"After I had the baby, my Constance, things got... weird. He was gone more. He was *always* gone a lot because he had a job that took him all over the place. He traveled a lot, right?"

I nod but don't say anything.

"It got to where he'd come home for one day a week, and then even less. And he became abusive. He didn't want to have much of anything to do with the baby, and he said he'd come around more if I dropped some weight and didn't look like a cow."

I close my eyes and take a long, deep breath. God, he was a piece of shit. I mean, he was cheating on me with this woman, but still a piece of shit to speak to her that way.

"He ended up calling off the engagement, and Constance didn't see him often. He promised to come around but always broke those promises. He missed birthdays and holidays. Of course, now I realize that he was spending the holidays with you."

"Sometimes," I whisper as Cam sits next to me once more and holds my hand. I turn to him. "Is the plumber doing his thing?"

"He's already gone. Turned out to be an easy fix."

"Oh. Okay. Sorry, go ahead."

"A few months ago, Constance asked if she could call her daddy. I called his number, and it had been disconnected. I don't know why, but I had a bad feeling and decided to do some digging." Heather rubs a hand over her face. "I found his obituary. And my God, it was all about a man I didn't know. The name fit, but the details? Everything was wrong. I couldn't imagine how he could have a life in Washington. A *wife*. I was just...stunned."

"It took you *months* to try to find him? You have a child. Are you saying that it never occurred to you that you hadn't heard from him or received any money?"

"No, it didn't. He didn't pay child support, and like I said, we would go months without a word. I moved on with my life, and Connie and I are doing well. I even met someone. But when I found the obituary, I just couldn't stop thinking about it. I slept with a married man. I had a *child* with him. And all the while, he was lying to me."

I take a long, deep breath and glance over at Cam and then back at Heather.

"What do you want to know?"

Heather blinks at me and then laughs a little. "You know, you'd think I would have made a list by now. I've had so many questions pop into my head over the past few months, and now that I'm sitting here with you, not even one of them comes to mind. Any except *how*. How did he do this for so long?"

"Okay. First of all, I'm just going to tell you what I know, which is both a lot and not enough all at the same time. I know that doesn't make any sense, but it's true."

"Well, I know *nothing*, so I'm all ears."

"I married him just out of high school. You probably met him that summer."

"So, he wasn't twenty-two when I met him."

I blink at her and then laugh. "No. No, he would have been eighteen. He must have had a fake ID. How old were you?"

"Twenty-five," she says.

"From what I can tell, Joey had girlfriends all over the country. He did travel for work, although given everything, I don't know what that work was. Maybe it wasn't work at all, who knows. He traveled, and he fucked around. After he died, I found roughly twenty-five women for sure that I know he was with during our marriage, and there may be more. Hell, one of them even showed up to the funeral and accosted me after it."

"Oh my God," Heather whispers. Her blue eyes round in horror, and her hands shake as she presses them to her mouth. "Maggie, I'm so sorry."

"I'm fine," I say honestly. "I really am. Now, how have you been getting by if Joey never gave you child support?"

"I have a job," she replies. "And I have family. My

fiancé is amazing. Once we're married, he'll adopt Connie."

"Good." I nod slowly. "That's good. I'm glad for you, I really am. Heather, Joey left you money."

Her hands fall to her lap. "What?"

"He hid money. A *lot* of it. And on all of the accounts, he listed you and Constance as the beneficiaries."

She frowns and shakes her head. "He never said anything about any money. Is it a small life insurance policy or something?"

"No. It's several accounts of no less than two hundred thousand dollars each."

I watch her face carefully. I want to see the reaction.

I want to see if she already knows.

Her mouth opens, and then she simply reduces to tears. She folds in on herself, sobbing, and before I realize what I'm doing, I hurry over to her and pat her back.

My eyes find Cam's. He looks frustrated, like I shouldn't have told her everything I know, but what do I have to lose?

"Why didn't he tell me?" she sobs. "Why save that money for our baby and not tell me about it? There were months that I had to ask my parents for help because I just couldn't make ends meet. And all this time…"

She breaks down again, and all I can do is rub her back. Cam passes us a box of tissues.

"Okay, I'm okay." She wipes at her face and sits back, dabbing at her eyes some more. "I'm sorry, I wasn't expecting that. I didn't know he was rich."

"He wasn't," I reply simply. "I don't know how he got the money. But it's yours. I'll get you the information so you can claim it."

She blows out a breath, and I return to my seat next to Cam.

"How are you so calm?" she asks me.

"I've had two years to get used to this," I remind her. "Two years to heal. You only recently found out about it all."

"Did he hit you, too?" she asks me and then looks at the floor.

"Did Joey Lemon hit you, Heather?"

She bites her lip and then nods, turning her blue gaze back to me. "Yeah. Yeah, he did. But when he did it in front of Constance, I stood up for myself and told him I wouldn't put up with that from him." She shrugs. "We never saw him again. My baby lost her father because of me."

"Bullshit." I say it hard and firm. "Her father was an abusive prick, and she's better off without him, no matter if he was still alive or not. And I'm not sorry for saying that."

"I know." She sighs again. "I know it. But I still feel guilty. And I know that's stupid, too. If my best friend told me any of this, I'd tell her the same thing. So, why does it feel different when it happens to you?"

"Because the abuser makes you feel like it's your fault. Joey was a master manipulator. He could be a complete jerk and then turn around and charm you."

"That's true." She checks her watch. "I took up longer than fifteen minutes."

"It's okay. Now that I'm calm, it's okay. I'm just anxious not to have reminders of that man popping up every single day of my life."

"I live with one," she says kindly. "And while I wouldn't trade her for anything in the world, she is a daily reminder. She looks just like him. And, speaking of, I have to get home to her. I've been here on the island for three days. I just mustered up the courage to come by this morning, and it's a good thing I did because my flight to Dallas leaves later this afternoon."

"If you leave me your email address, I'll get all of the banking information to you."

"Call her with it," Cam suggests. "You shouldn't send banking information through email. It's not secure."

"I'll call you with it," I amend. "Oh, and here."

I hurry into my little office-slash-storage room, where I keep my files and grab a file folder.

"You'll need an *official* death certificate, I think, to claim the accounts. I have about fifty of them. Here you go."

I pass the certificate over to Heather, and she stares down at it.

"He's dead," she says simply.

"And buried." I tilt my head as I watch her, an idea forming in my head. "Do you want to see where he's buried?"

Her head comes up and she nods. "You know what? I do. Yes, I do."

I turn to Cameron, who's been quiet this whole time. I'll ask him later what he's been thinking, but for now, I'm going to finish this.

I'm going to finish it all.

"Come on, let's go."

"I'll see you later. I'm going to Kane's," Cam says and leans over to kiss my cheek. "Call me when you're done."

"Okay. Thank you."

"Thank you," Heather echoes.

"I don't have a car," I announce after Cameron leaves.

"I do," she says. "I'll drive. You give directions."

"Deal."

"WE HAVE to park here and then walk the rest of the way," I tell Heather as I point to the best space for her to pull off the single-lane road that winds through the cemetery. "He's just over there."

We get out of the car, and I breathe in the clean spring air. I love springtime on the island. The worst days of clouds and rain are starting to dissipate, and

I've been promised at least a couple of months of sunshine.

Today is one of those sunny days. The sky is clear, and we can even smell the salt water from here. I lead Heather through the gravestones toward the plot that I haven't visited since the day of Joey's funeral.

But if I'm going to wrap this all up today, this is a good way to do it. I'd thought yesterday was the last of it, but I was wrong.

And, as horrified as I was when I realized who Heather was, I'm not sorry that she's here. It's one more thing to wrap up.

Hopefully, and I've got my fingers crossed, this is the very last thing.

"Some of these stones are beautiful," Heather says as she drags her fingertips over the top of a grave.

"Joey's parents went all out," I inform Heather as we approach the grave we're looking for.

"Whoa," Heather says.

The headstone is at least five feet tall, with a photo of Joey inlaid in it. His full name, birth date, and death date are engraved, and below that is a damn long epitaph.

"Why does it look like they worshiped him?" Heather asks.

"Because they did," I confirm. "They hated me and blamed me for his death. He was an only child."

"He told me that his parents were long dead," Heather confides. "I asked him if Constance should

169

meet his parents, and he said they died when he was a kid."

"Ever the storyteller," I say, shaking my head. "His parents are very much alive. Last I heard, they moved off the island, though. And if you want my advice—"

"I do."

"I wouldn't tell them about Constance. They're controlling, and I think they would try to interfere in your life in ways that you wouldn't welcome."

"But she's their *granddaughter.*" Heather scrunches up her nose. "It feels wrong to keep her from them."

"Your call," I reply, my hands up in surrender. "But they raised Joey, and I'm not sure that's a good thing."

"Yeah, well, you're not wrong. I'll think about it, do some research. I don't usually make rash decisions."

Heather squats next to the stone, just inches from Joey's picture.

"You were a son of a bitch, Joey Lemon. I'm not sorry you're dead, and that makes me feel guilty because I was taught better than that. You didn't deserve Constance. She's so much better without you, and Rob is going to be an awesome father to her. The father you never could be."

Heather stands and takes a couple of steps back.

"I don't know if he can hear me, but it feels good to say the words."

"I've told him off...I don't know how many times since he died. It does feel good."

To my utter surprise, Heather reaches out and takes

my hand. We stand, side by side, staring down at what's left of the man we both loved once.

"I know it's weird, but I'd like to stay in touch," she says.

"It's a little weird," I admit. "But I think I like you."

Heather laughs, and I join her. Before long, we're laughing so hard, we're both wiping away tears. My side aches. I might pee myself.

But, damn, it feels so good.

"My family has a habit of adopting people," I say when I can breathe again and am wiping at the tears on my cheeks. "I know that you and Constance would be welcome here any time."

"Thank you."

Heather turns away from Joey, and I think turning her back to the man is symbolic.

Yeah, I like her.

"Maybe I'll bring Connie here someday. When she's a little older. She asks about Joey. Not often, but sometimes it's like she'll have a memory of something and ask questions. When she's older, I'll bring her here and tell her the story."

"When she's *much* older," I advise as we walk back to the car. "Because I'm twenty-eight, and I don't fully understand it."

"You're only twenty-eight?" Heather asks and then laughs again. "That's right, I was way more of a cradle robber than I thought I was. Just another part of the story. At least, he was of age, and I didn't break any laws—in that respect, anyway."

"I don't think you broke any laws," I say after we've lowered ourselves into the car and fastened our seat belts. "I'm sorry I never spoke to you before."

"Are you kidding? I would have told me to go fuck myself."

"I might have said that under my breath when I hung up on you."

"As it should have been." She starts the car. "Wanna grab a coffee on the way back to your house?"

"Hell, yes."

The drive into town is quick, and Heather pulls up to my favorite drive-thru coffee stand. We place our order and then head to my house.

My ma and da are sitting on the porch swing as if they just hang out there every day.

When Heather stops the car, I turn to her.

"Want to meet my parents?"

Her eyes widen, and she snorts out a laugh. "Hell, why not?"

"They're nice. You'll like them."

When we climb the stairs with our coffees, I smile at my parents.

"Hi, guys. This is Heather. Heather, this is Fiona and Tom O'Callaghan, my parents."

"Oh, darlin'," Ma croons and stands, but rather than hugging *me*, she wraps her arms around Heather. "Are you all right, then?"

"I'm…I'm fine, thank you." Heather pats Ma's back. "It's nice to meet you."

"I told you," I say as I sit next to Da and rest my head on his shoulder, "we tend to just bring people into the fold. And it looks like you've been folded."

"I would think you'd be angry with me," Heather says as fresh tears fill her eyes.

"And what for?" Da demands. "T'wasn't your fault that Joey Lemon was a lowlife, was it? And you have a wee one to care for on top of it."

"Did you bring her with you?" Ma asks, her voice full of hope.

"No, she's in Texas."

"Probably for the best," Ma says with a nod. "If you come with us to the pub, we'll feed you full of whatever your heart desires."

Heather laughs and shakes her head. "I'm sorry, I have to get to the airport. But I'm so grateful that I got to meet you."

She turns to me as I stand once more.

"Thank you. For not kicking me out and for helping me."

"You're welcome. Just call when you get home, and I'll get you all of the information you need."

Heather says goodbye, and once she's driven away, I sit between my parents on the swing. Ma takes my hand, and Da kisses my cheek.

"She seems very nice," Ma says at last.

"Yeah. She is. And he hurt her like he did me.

Worse, really, because she had a baby, and he didn't care at all."

I tell them about Heather's fiancé, and Da nods.

"They'll be taken care of, and that's all that matters."

"I hate to say this out loud, in case I jinx it," I say and squeeze Ma's hand, "but I think that's the last of it. I can finally move on with my life."

"And it's about time," Ma says. "Because you still have a lot of life to live, my sweet girl."

CHAPTER 13

~CAMERON~

"*I*'m dreading this," Maggie says as I pull into the car lot in Seattle.

"Obviously. You dragged your feet getting ready to come here today, and I think they're going to close in about three hours."

"If I can't buy a car in less than three hours, there's a huge problem. *Huge.*"

"It's not a quick process, you know."

She looks over at me with disgust, and I can't help but laugh.

"Come on. It won't be so bad. You can afford pretty much anything you want here."

Maggie sighs and gets out of my car as if she's being dragged to the dentist for a root canal. Before we can even start looking at the rows of available vehicles for sale, a salesman comes walking toward us.

"Hi there, how can I help you today?"

"I need a car," Maggie says.

"You came to the right place," he replies and then offers his hand to *me*. "I'm Roland."

"Uh, Cam. Maggie is your customer. I'm just here for moral support."

"Nice to meet you, Maggie," Roland says. "So, what are you looking for?"

"Literally anything that runs," she replies. "I don't care other than that."

Roland presses his lips together and then looks at me.

I shrug.

Good luck, buddy.

"Do you prefer a sedan or an SUV?"

"Don't care."

"Any particular color?"

"Nope."

Roland laughs and rubs his hand over his neck. "Okay. Let's start with this. What will you be using it for, on a daily basis?"

"Pretty much just going back and forth to work, but I live on one of the islands, so we do get unpredictable weather."

"Okay, that's a good start. An all-wheel-drive SUV might be good. But a smaller one, I think."

"Yeah, I don't need a tank," she agrees. "But all-wheel-drive sounds good."

"Great, we have a place to start. Let's look over here."

Roland steers us a couple of rows over to a line of sleek, brand-new vehicles.

"Great, pick one, and I'll take it."

Now Roland laughs and shakes his head. "No, that's your job, Maggie."

"As long as it starts when I want it to and doesn't die on me, I'm not picky. Oh, but I do like red."

"Let's start with the red one, then." He explains all about heated seats and backup cameras and a bunch of things that I'm sure Maggie doesn't give two fucks about.

"What about a moonroof?" Roland asks her.

Maggie looks up. "There isn't one."

"Not in this vehicle, but it's an option. Also, have you thought about lane assist, which cruise control you'd like, if you would like a heated steering wheel—"

"Whoa." Maggie holds up her hands and stares at Roland as if he just told her to get ready for the biggest test of her life. "A heated *steering wheel*?"

"That's right."

"I don't need any of those things. I don't care if I have to use a key to unlock the door, and I have to roll the windows up and down by hand as long as the engine starts."

"I don't think I even have a vehicle on this lot with manual windows," Roland says with a laugh. "How often do you buy yourself a new car? I can tell that you're not an every-other-year kind of person."

"No, I think I purchased the last one eight years ago."

"Exactly," Roland says, and I smile. I see where he's going with this, and I couldn't agree more. If I were making the purchase, I'd make sure she had every bell and whistle possible. "So, why shouldn't you get all of the amenities offered, all of the safety features, and enjoy them for the next eight years? You can plug your phone in and listen to any music you'd like, or—"

"Wait." Maggie turns in the seat, excited. "I can listen to the music on my *phone?*"

"That's right. You can plug it in or use Bluetooth."

"Plugging it in sounds easier."

Roland smiles. "It is. You can also use the maps for directions if you want."

"Okay, maybe the fancy car is starting to sound good. I think I even want the moonroof thing."

"Great. I don't have that specific vehicle on the lot, but I can have it transferred from another location by tomorrow morning."

"Okay." Maggie hops out of the car and walks around the vehicle once. "And I want it in red."

"We can do that," Roland confirms. "If you'll just come inside with me, we'll get everything started."

"I'm paying cash," she informs him as we set off for the office. "So don't bother with financing and all the other stuff. This should be quick and easy."

I smirk behind her.

Famous last words.

"Why did that still take another ninety minutes?" Maggie demands as we drive away from the dealership.

"There's a lot of paperwork involved in buying a car."

"But I'm paying *cash*," she insists. "I should just write the check and walk out with the car. As if I'm buying a couch or some chips at the store."

"You're cute."

She narrows her eyes at me dangerously.

"You know there are registration and warranty things. You were there."

"It's a pain in the ass," she grumbles. "But at least when we come back over in the morning, all I have to do is sign for it, and we can leave."

Maggie glances around and then turns back to me.

"Why aren't we headed for the ferry?"

"Because we aren't getting on a ferry," I reply. "We'll stay in Seattle tonight and head back after we get your car tomorrow."

"A mini-vacation," she says. "Fun. Let's get Italian for dinner."

"I think we can manage that."

"Do you ever wish you lived in the city?" I ask as Maggie holds my hand, and we walk from the restaurant, where we stuffed ourselves with bread and pasta, toward the hotel. It's a beautiful evening, so we decided to hoof it. I'm glad we did because I have to work this food off.

"Not really," she says. "Why, do you?"

"Sometimes, I wish we had some of the conveniences closer—like the airport, restaurants, and stuff like that."

"Seattle isn't that far from the island."

"Far enough that it's a pain in the ass sometimes. Don't get me wrong, I love the island."

"If you could just snap your fingers and live anywhere in the world, where would that be?" she asks.

"I don't know. I've been almost everywhere there is to go, and I don't know that there's anything better than this. Maybe Ireland."

Her face lights up. "Really?"

"I do love it there."

"I do, too. That's the only other place I would live, too. But I don't think I could move away from the family, especially now that everyone's having babies. I don't like being out of the loop."

"Your parents are good at having a foot in both places," I remind her.

"They're retired," she says with a shrug. "Someday, I'll retire there, too."

"Are you still thinking that you're content at the pub?"

"I love the pub," she says slowly. "It's what I know, and I am good at my job."

"You're great at it," I agree.

"But I've been thinking more about what Leo offered. The possibility of singing with his band is the opportunity of a lifetime. But wouldn't it make me a hypocrite if I went?"

I glance down at her and frown. "How so?"

"All I've done for the past two years is complain that you're never home. And now I'm considering a job that takes me literally all over the world, and I don't know how long the tour runs. It could be weeks or years. I think P!nk's last tour lasted four years."

"It doesn't make you a hypocrite," I reply. "I think that if it appeals to you, and if they offer, you should try it. I'll be here. I'm sure I can join you here and there."

"You'd do that?"

I bring her hand up to my lips. "Of course, I would. I can work anywhere, Maggie."

We walk into the hotel and to the elevators. Once the doors close, I glance over at her. She smiles at me.

"What are you thinking?" I ask, recognizing the lust in her emerald eyes.

"Have you ever wondered what it would be like to have sex in an elevator?"

And just like that, I'm hard and ready for her. I cup her jawline in one hand and kiss her long and hard, then pull back as her phone rings.

"Just when my deepest sexy fantasy is about to be realized," she mutters and pulls her phone out of her pocket. "It's my ma. Hello? You're kidding. How did you know—? Oh." She glances at me as the elevator doors open, then follows me down the hall to our room. "Well, we aren't planning to be back until tomorrow afternoon, but I could probably ask Cam to take us back—okay. You're sure? Thanks, Ma. Just let me know if you change your mind. Love you. Bye."

"What happened?" I ask as I unlock the door, and we walk into the room. Maggie blows out a long breath.

"My fridge went out," she says and scratches her fingertips into her scalp. "It must have happened right after we left because Ma popped over to borrow one of my stockpots, and when she went to look in the fridge for some chicken stock, she found it dead."

I blink at her.

"I thought your house was fairly new?"

"It's almost ten years old, and I'm sure none of the appliances were ever replaced before I bought it. But still. When it rains, it pours. At least, I can afford to fix it."

Her head comes up, and she looks at me with wonder.

"I can *afford* to fix it, Cam. Just a week ago, I would have been in full panic mode, but I don't have to panic. I mean, yeah, I'll lose some food, but I can replace it. I didn't realize until now what a luxury that is."

"You're right," I agree, remembering days as a kid when my dad couldn't always afford to keep the lights on. "It's a good feeling to have that buffer."

"Now I know how the others feel, and it's damn nice. I've never been one to assume that because all of my siblings are successful, that they owe me anything. That they should just automatically jump in and rescue me. I was raised to take care of myself but always know that my family would help me if I needed them, you know?"

"And yet, you never ask for help. Why is that, Mary Margaret? Any one of them, me included, would have helped you with that damn hot water heater."

She chews her lip then walks over to the window and looks out at the water.

She does that often. She should live closer to the beach where she can see the view. I know she'd love it.

"I don't know why."

And that's not the truth. There are moments when I still feel like Maggie holds back while confiding in me. Keeps herself from opening up all the way. And it's damn frustrating.

I join her at the window, wrap my arms around her from behind, and silently stand with her, staring out at the water. The sun has already slid behind the horizon, and the sky is ablaze in orange and pink as boats litter the Sound before us.

"Someday, you'll open up to me without me having to pry it out of you."

"I—" She sighs and doesn't complete the thought. "I'll get better."

And that's all I can ask.

My hand slips up under her light sweater until I feel the warm flesh against my palm. Her head falls back against my shoulder in surrender.

I *love* how she gives herself over to me so easily. Physically, she's as free as can be with me, but emotionally? Well, we're not quite there yet.

But I'm determined to get there.

"You have the softest skin," I murmur as I cup her breasts and tease her nipples over her bra. "And you smell delicious."

"I smell like pasta," she says with a smile in her voice. "And probably garlic bread."

"Delicious," I repeat softly.

"Good enough to eat?"

She's teasing, but it's no joke to me. I nip her ear, then take her hand and pull her with me to the bed, where I don't even undress her before urging her back onto the mattress.

"Hold on to the headboard," I instruct her.

"This again?" Her pink lips tip up into an excited grin. "There's nothing for me to hold on to, Cam."

Hmm, she's right. This hotel doesn't take certain... tastes into consideration.

"Okay, grasp on to the pillow, on either side of your head. And don't—"

"Don't let go," she finishes for me.

I narrow my eyes on her and boost up until I'm at eye level with her, my face inches from hers.

"Do you think this is the time to be sassy, Mary Margaret?" My voice is firm and leaves no room for argument.

But she doesn't look afraid, which pleases me. One red eyebrow cocks.

"Apparently, not. Should I call you *sir*?"

My cock twitches. I brush my nose over hers and wait until she grips the pillow in both hands before pulling her sweater up and loosely wrapping it over her head so she can't see well but can still breathe.

"If you get uncomfortable, just tell me, and I'll move the sweater. But don't let go. You need to trust me. Understood?"

"Yes, sir," she whispers, and I immediately smile.

She can't see me.

"Good girl," I say in her ear, then kiss my way down to her perfect little breasts. I unfasten her bra and move the cups out of the way so I can tease her pink nipples. Once they're wet from my tongue, I blow on them and watch in satisfaction as they tighten.

Next, I make my way to her jeans. With a flick of my wrist, they come unfastened, and I tug the denim down her gorgeous, curvy hips, unveiling a scrap of blue cotton covering the promised land.

Her flesh erupts in goosebumps at the exposure to the air, and her hips circle when I push one finger under the elastic at her thigh and follow it inward as if her heat is a magnet.

"Oh, damn it," she moans and shifts her legs. "Cameron, you're such a tease."

"I didn't say you could talk."

She chuckles and then presses her lips together, trying to muffle a moan when I slide the finger deeper under her panties.

"You can, however, moan, gasp, groan, and scream my name to your heart's content."

"Oh, God," she moans and makes me smile once more.

Fucking hell, she's amazing. Everything I've ever wanted in a woman. In a partner.

And when my finger slips effortlessly between her wet folds, she gasps.

"Cam!"

CHAPTER 14

~MAGGIE~

*H*e's trying to kill me. That's the only explanation for the no-talking, no-seeing, no-moving stuff.

Because it's hot as hell. Figuratively *and* literally, and I don't want him to stop.

Does this mean I'm submissive? I don't even know. I've only read books and watched movies about this stuff, and I always rolled my eyes. I would have said that I'd punch any man who *dared* to tell me whether or not I could speak.

But when it comes from Cam, a man that I trust—hell, *love*—it's the hottest thing I've ever heard.

Not to mention, the way he growls, "Good girl," makes me *want* to be a good girl. And that's ludicrous. But true.

Good God, I'm losing my mi-i-ind. "Shit!"

Cam laughs, the sadistic jerk, as he taps on my clit,

and I see stars. It doesn't matter that I'm not allowed to talk. I couldn't form a sentence to save my life anyway.

My hips move in invitation, my heels digging into the mattress, and my hands white-knuckled on the pillow as Cam does intoxicating things to me. I've *never* had a man pay so much attention to the details.

"You have a little freckle right…here." He presses a kiss right next to my labia. "And one here." Another kiss on the other side.

I want to remind him that I have freckles *everywhere*, but I hold the words in and sigh in delight when his mouth covers me, and he really gets down to business.

Who knew how *satisfying* sex could be? Not me. Not until Cameron. I didn't know that electricity could shoot through me with just one touch or that memories of these moments could do the same days later.

Even when he's not touching me!

How is that even possible?

"Cam!" I reach out for him blindly, but he takes my hand, kisses it, and returns it to the pillow.

"Keep your hands up here," he says sternly.

"Or what?" I whisper, then bite my lip in the silence that follows.

Shit.

"Or we stop."

I immediately clamp my hand back onto the pillow and shut my big mouth because I do *not* want him to stop.

"Is that what you want?" he murmurs in my ear.

I shake my head no.

"You can use your words to answer."

"No. I don't want you to stop." I swallow hard. "Sir."

Cameron laughs—*laughs!*—and then gets back to work. How does he know that I like to be touched just like that? That I need to be caressed, right *there*?

How does he know me so well?

These are questions to file away for later.

Finally, I hear his clothes rustling as he strips out of them, and then the bed dips between my legs as Cam kneels there. God, I want to see him. I want to watch his blue eyes darken as he slips inside of me, and I want to see them close because he's overcome from the sensation of us joining.

I want to watch *everything.*

And he must agree because with the head of his cock poised at my opening, he tugs my sweater over my head so I can see him.

With that dark blue gaze locked on mine, he pushes inside of me and stops when he's balls-deep.

"You're everything."

Two words that hold more meaning than anything I've ever been told in my life.

"Please, can I touch you?"

He narrows his eyes, but I shake my head. "Please. I need to."

Cam's expression softens, and then he takes one

hand off the pillow and kisses it. "Touch me, babe. Anywhere you want."

And so, I do. His chest, down that tight stomach, and when I brush my fingertips over his shaft as he moves in and out of me, he mutters, "Christ."

Emboldened, I do it again, and when he falls over me, resting on his elbows, I grip on to his firm ass.

He brushes his thumb over my lower lip, and I stick my tongue out to lick it, then bite the pad.

"Fuck, Mary Margaret." His voice is thick and raspy. "Yes, you are."

He tips his forehead to mine, and we're lost, falling into an abyss that isn't dark at all but rather bursting with light and sound.

Later, when our skin and the sheets have cooled, and our heartbeats return to normal, I look over at him in the dark and see that his eyes are open and on me.

"Do I need a safe word?" I blurt out.

He raises an eyebrow again. "If you feel like you do, then we should have one. Did you feel like you needed to use one just now?"

He scoots closer and pulls me to him, brushing his hand through my hair.

"No, I didn't. But I never expected you to be so... assertive in bed, either."

"Let's clear some things up," he says quietly. "You don't have to call me *sir*. I'm not a Dominant."

"But you *are* dominant," I say with no censure in my voice. "And I don't mind that, much to my surprise. In fact, I think it's pretty hot. But what if there's a moment when I want you to stop, but you've told me not to talk?"

"Then you say, 'Stop, Cam.' And I'll stop. If you're not feeling it, or if you're uncomfortable, say so. We're not in a club, we're not in the middle of a scene. We're making love, Mags."

"True. Yeah, okay, I like that. You did listen when I said I needed to touch you."

"Yes, exactly like that." He kisses my fingertips. "Just tell me what you need, and we'll make it happen. I'll never hurt you."

"I know. I know that. Have you always been this bossy? Wait." I hold up a hand, shushing him. "I don't want to know."

He laughs and kisses my nose. "I don't think anything in my life has been like what I feel when I'm with you, and that's the truth."

"Same." That was the perfect answer. I lean in and kiss him softly. "Same here."

"We should sleep," he says. "Especially if we're going to go shopping for a fridge before we pick up the car."

"I'm begging you." I cup his face in my hands and stare intently into his eyes. "Please, for the love of all that's holy, will you do it? Will you just buy me a fridge? I'll pay you back for it. I don't want to pick it out, Cam. I don't care as long as it's big and has a freezer and an ice maker. *Please.*"

He sighs but nods and kisses my lips once more.

"Okay. I'll pick one out and arrange for it to be delivered. But don't complain about the one I choose, okay?"

"Deal. Absolutely. I will never, *ever* complain about it."

"I should get that on video to show you later."

"I have a better idea."

I push him onto his back and straddle him, grinning when I feel him harden beneath me.

"That's definitely a better idea."

I LOVE THIS CAR.

I might want to marry this car.

I didn't even want to get out of it on the ferry while we rode over to the island.

I pull into my driveway just ahead of Cam with my music blaring. He parks behind me, and I push the button to turn off the engine, then hurry out of my brand-spanking-new vehicle and run to my man, jumping into his arms to hug him close.

"I listened to the music on my *phone*!" I inform him and kiss his cheek. "My ass was warm, and my hands were warm, and I could see the blue sky if I wanted to!"

"So, you like it then?"

"I *love* it. I'm not even mad anymore that it took another hour at the dealership this morning."

"Good. Let's go in and clean up the fridge mess. The new one will be here this afternoon."

I frown as he sets me on my feet. "Wait. *This* afternoon?"

"Yes."

He's walking away from me, toward the front door, and I have to pick up the pace to keep up with him.

"How? We've been busy all day. How did you find the time to get me a fridge?"

I unlock the door, and when we step inside, I have to cover my nose with my hand.

"Oh, God. How did it get so smelly so fast?"

"Food goes bad," Cam says grimly. "It's called bacteria. Start opening windows, and I'll get the trash bags."

"We can't open the door of that thing," I protest, breathing into the sleeve of my sweater. "Cam, can't we just throw it all away in one fell swoop?"

"I don't think the appliance company will haul it away with the food still inside," he says. "Unfortunately, we have to clear it out. You can do it. I'm sure you've seen worse."

"I work in a bar. Of course, I've seen worse. Maybe."

I hurry around the house, opening all the windows and doors, flipping on overhead fans. I even drag out the big box fan I use in the summertime.

I don't have A/C.

With the fan on full blast and with both of us wearing gloves and armed with trash bags, Cam and I hurry to empty the fridge and freezer of all their contents.

"I'll never look at turkey the same again," I say as I try to breathe through my mouth.

"I don't think I'll eat stew anytime soon, either," Cam agrees as we hurry out to the dumpster with the first few bags, then rush back inside to fill two more. "That's it. Let's haul these out, and then we'll muscle this thing out to the porch."

I hurry behind him and toss away the food. When we're back inside, Cam and I manage to work the fridge out of its space between the wall and my kitchen counter and get it out onto the front porch.

"It already smells better in here," I say with a sigh. "But it might take a day or two to get back to normal."

"I bet it's much better in a couple of hours. We'll spray some air freshener."

"Should we haul the garbage somewhere?" I ask. "It's going to smell up the neighborhood."

"When is your garbage day?"

"Not until Tuesday, and today's Thursday."

Cam cringes. "I'll call the garbage company and ask if they'll make a special trip over here in the morning."

"They do stuff like that?"

"I don't know. I'm going to ask them."

Cam pulls out his phone to make the call, and I go hunt down the air freshener.

I spray every room. According to the bottle, my

house is going to smell like a spring meadow. And it will if it's the last thing I do.

"Good news," Cam says when he finds me in the office, spraying. "They'll come by today on their last route."

"Well, that's handy. Thanks."

"I know you've been hard at work spraying that stuff, but now the house just smells like a rotten meadow."

I sigh in defeat. "Yuck."

"It's okay. We'll stay at my place tonight, and we'll leave the windows open all night to air it out. It's safe here, it'll be okay."

"Okay. That should work. Besides, maybe some of what we smell is coming from outside."

"Very possible. I think I hear the delivery truck."

By the time my new fridge is in and running, and the old one is long gone, I've almost forgotten about the smell.

"This is an *expensive* appliance," I say as I turn to Cameron, who wears an expression of absolute innocence.

"You said you wouldn't complain."

"But did you have to get the most expensive one they had?"

"It's not. They didn't have that one in stock, and I knew you wouldn't want to wait."

"Ha-ha." I open the stainless-steel appliance and

sigh in happiness. "It *is* gorgeous. And it'll hold so much stuff!"

"I know you love to cook, and you need a good fridge. You often cook for the pub ahead of time, so you should have an *almost* top-of-the-line appliance."

"Yeah, okay. You're right. So, I have a new car, a new fridge, and my hot water heater is fixed. I think, as long as I'm not about to jinx it, that things should go back to normal now."

"That's three things, so I think you're safe."

"Yeah, these things do happen in threes." I walk to my bedroom and start packing a bag. "I'll just bring enough stuff for overnight, and then we'll reassess."

"You can stay for as long as you need."

"That's really nice of you." I grin when he hugs me from behind as I've learned he loves to do. "You're so selfless."

"That's me. They call me *Selfless Cameron*."

I snort and pluck my phone off the bed when it starts to ring. "Hello?"

"Hey, are you back?"

"I am, and I have a fancy new car," I inform Maeve. "What are you doing?"

"We're hosting family dinner tonight. Keegan's even closing down the pub early so we can all get together at once."

"Awesome. What can I bring?"

"Nothing, we have it handled. Oh, bring Cameron."

"I already planned to." I look at the man in question,

who's watching me from the doorway where he's leaning on the doorjamb, looking all kinds of sexy. "What time?"

"Dinner's at six, but you can come anytime. I think most of the guys are planning to play out in Hunter's gym. He got some new toys. Oh, and Hunter's parents are here, too."

"You have a full house. We'll head that way in just a few so I can help with everything."

"Thanks. I want to see your new car, too."

"I'll be sure to drive it over so I can show it off. It's shiny. And it heats my ass."

"Fancy," she says and then hangs up.

"How do you feel about family dinner at Maeve's?" I ask Cam.

"I think it's the perfect opportunity for you to show off your new wheels."

"That's what I said." I zip my bag closed and turn to him. "Shall we go? I want to go over and help Maeve and Ma with dinner. I know the other girls are there, too, but it's a lot of work. And, I'll be honest, I just want to hang out with them."

"At last, you tell me what you want. I'm ready. Let's get out of this stinky house."

I laugh and lead the way to the front, locking the door behind us. Cam stows my bag in my new car.

"Want me to follow you to your place so we can leave your car there and just take this one to Maeve's?"

"Sounds like a plan."

CHAPTER 15

~CAMERON~

"*A*nd that's about it." I push my hand through my hair and glance around at the guys, who have all assembled in Hunter's gym, where I've just filled them all in on the past few days.

Of course, I left out the part about the best sex of my damn life, even though I'm headed toward forty, but Maggie's older brothers, not to mention her father, don't want to hear that part.

"You've been busy," Hunter says. "Is your head still whirling?"

"Pretty much," I confirm.

"That's a *lot* of money," Shawn adds. "And it pisses me right off that it took her two years to find it. That fucker."

A fresh wave of guilt hits me because I knew about the account all along.

But I couldn't tell her.

"Well, she has it now," Kane says. "And wasted no time getting the things she needs, which is a good start."

"She wouldn't choose a fridge," I inform them. "She insisted I do it. Has she always been this indecisive?"

"No," Kane replies.

"Not until she married *The Lemon*," Shawn adds. "After, whenever we asked for her opinion on something, she would say, *'Whatever is easiest is fine.'*"

I narrow my eyes as it all starts to make sense. Why didn't I think of it before?

"So, she's not good at asking for help or for things that she really wants. She'll just go with the status quo, even if that means that she takes something she doesn't like."

"What a prick," Hunter mutters and shakes his head. "So, in other words, he just always got his way, and Maggie put up with it."

"Yeah, so now she's used to that," Keegan says. "She just goes with the flow, and anyone who knew her as a kid knows that's not *her*."

"My Maggie is a fireball," Tom adds. "She's always been opinionated and not afraid to voice those opinions. Sometimes, that's still the case, but not when it comes to herself. She'll get better as time goes on. It's glad I am that my girl had you to lean on in all of this," Tom says as he claps his hand on my shoulder. "Thank you for helping her."

"She did it all," I say, meaning every word. "I was

just there as moral support. She stood up for herself at that bank and handled Heather perfectly. She loves the new car."

"So, here's the million-dollar question," Keegan says as he lifts a dumbbell and curls his biceps, trying out the new equipment. "When are you going to pop the question?"

Five sets of eyes turn to me, and I can only grin. "If I thought she'd say yes, I'd ask her today. But we're not there yet. She's had a busy week, and she's finally starting to put all of the shit she went through with *The Lemon* to rest and move on. We have time, you know? But I will ask when the time is right."

"Aww, that's so sweet," Hunter says with a grin. "Look at us, all a bunch of Mushy Marcias over a bunch of women and babies. And that's not a bad thing."

"As it should be," Tom says with a wink. "Because life wouldn't be worth living if we didn't have them with us."

"I didn't think I'd ever marry," Kane admits, shaking his head. "Wasn't even on my radar. I was happy out in that barn by myself, marking time by how much glass I blew. Until I saw Anastasia sitting on that bench in my museum, and it was like everything in the world was suddenly in color. Does that make me a Mushy Marcia? Aye, it does, and that doesn't bother me in the least."

"Same goes," Hunter says with a grin, then looks out

the window when we hear a car door close. "Well, the kid showed up, after all."

"Who's the kid?" I ask, joining him at the window.

"Rachel's been dating this boy, Brian Masterson."

"I know the Masterson boy," Keegan says with a nod. "It's a good family."

"I actually like him," Hunter admits as we all walk out of the gym and to the driveway where Brian just stepped out of his car. "But he doesn't need to know that yet."

"Hello, Mr. Meyers," Brian says with a brave smile. I can see that he's nervous, but he holds his hand out to shake Hunter's. "Thanks for inviting me here today."

The young man turns to all of us and keeps that brave smile in place.

"I'm Brian. I've been seeing Rachel."

"So we hear," Kane says and folds his arms over his chest. "How old are you?"

"Seventeen," Brian replies. "Rachel and I are in the same grade."

His eyes dart to the house as the nerves start to show more, but we don't move. We're here to check him out, make sure he's good enough for our girl.

"What do you plan to do after high school?" Shawn asks him.

"College, but I'm not sure where yet. I'll probably stay here in Washington."

"Have you ever been in trouble?" I ask him. "And

you best not lie because I can find out *anything* I want to know about you with the press of a few buttons."

"Uh, no. No, sir. I once got detention because I accidentally set fire to something in science class."

"Are you an arsonist?" Hunter demands. "Are you going to burn down my fucking house?"

"No." Brian laughs. "Of course, not."

"And do you plan to sleep with my niece?" Keegan asks.

Brian opens his mouth, then closes it again. Licks his lips. "Honestly, I don't know how to answer that. If I say no, you'll ask me what's wrong with her, when there's nothing at all wrong with her. She's awesome. If I say yes, you'll punch me in the face. So, there's no right answer, except to say I'll always be respectful, and I would never ask her to do something she doesn't want to do."

We glance at each other in surprise.

"I think *that* was the right answer," I say at last and clap him on the shoulder. "Come on. We'll go in and help out in the kitchen."

"Did I pass that test?" Brian whispers to me.

"So far. Don't fuck it up, and you'll stay alive."

"Ma usually kicks us out of the kitchen," Shawn says. "But I'd like to steal a bite of something. I'm starved."

"We brought an appetizer," Keegan informs his brother.

"Why didn't you say so?" Shawn says, and we file in

the back door of Maeve and Hunter's gorgeous house that sits on the cliffs overlooking the ocean.

This is exactly the type of place I envision Maggie wanting to live in. And if that's the case, I'll buy a house like this for her. Maeve will have ideas. And if the perfect house doesn't currently exist, I'll build her one.

We descend on the kitchen, making the women laugh. Fiona shoos Shawn away from the pot she has boiling on the stove, just as he predicted.

"Get out of my way, Shawn O'Callaghan," she says, but then she pats him gently on the cheek. "It's hungry you are, I'm sure. There are some goodies over there on the island to keep you at bay until we're done in here."

"Brian!" Rachel exclaims and hurries over to hug him. "Oh, God, were my uncles mean to you?"

"No," Brian assures her with a smile. "They're really nice."

"Right." Rachel narrows her eyes and glares at us all but then smiles. "They're just overprotective."

With a glance, I realize that Maggie's not in the kitchen, so I set off in search of her.

I find her with Maeve and Lexi in the living room. Before I can join them, I hear Maeve say, "I don't like the problems you're having with your house, especially because you live alone. I know you settled on that place, Maggie, because you couldn't afford what you wanted. Why don't you sell it and buy what you *really* want?"

"It's fine," Maggie replies, the way she always does, and my jaw firms in frustration. I'll be damned if this woman will continue to *settle*. She deserves so much more than that. "It suits my needs just fine. It's just appliances, Maeve. My roof didn't cave in like at your old house. My staircase isn't a rushing river."

"Just think about it," Lexi says. "You've always wanted something closer to the water, and now you can afford that. I know we could find you something beautiful."

"I want to know how it's going with The Cock," Lexi says, lowering her voice, and both of my eyebrows climb into my hairline in surprise.

Maggie giggles. "He's good. Like, *really* good. No complaints there. And not just in the bedroom, but in every way. We're enjoying each other, and he's so nice. And, yes, the sex is superb."

"Attagirl," Lexi says. "I told you, the bossiness is fun in the bedroom."

"You weren't wrong," Maggie says.

She's been telling her sisters about our sex life?

The idea has a smile spreading over my face. I know she confides in these women, and from the sound of it, she's happy. That's what I want.

It doesn't bother me at all if she talks to them about us.

"Mags?" I call out and round the corner into the room. "The food's in there," I announce and point toward the kitchen. "What are you ladies up to?"

"We heard all of you file in and knew we wouldn't be able to think through the noise," Lexi says with a smile as Maggie's face flushes, and Maeve clears her throat over a laugh. "Also, Fiona keeps shooing us away, even though we're just trying to help."

"She likes to fuss," Maeve says and presses a hand against her belly. "This one likes to kick."

"Oh, let me feel," Maggie says and pounces on her sister, pressing her face to Maeve's stomach. "Talk to Auntie Mags, little love. That's right, tell me all about it."

I smirk as Keegan comes into the room holding his daughter, Eve.

"Our family has grown odd," he decides and sways back and forth with the baby. "Isn't that right, wee one?"

"She's beautiful," I inform him and reach over to let the baby grab my finger. "And she has a firm grip."

"I'm reminded every time she reaches for my hair," Izzy says as she joins us. "I live my life in a ponytail these days."

"Tommy, you come here with that!" Anastasia yells as her son toddles into the room, running with a full-sized pickle in his pudgy little grasp. "You can't eat that whole thing. You'll make a huge mess."

We spend an hour, a full *hour*, laughing at the babies' antics, and I find myself holding a sleepy Eve, rocking her in the chair in a corner, watching the others.

"Hello, lovely girl. You are a sweetheart, aren't you?" Her green eyes are huge as she sucks on her pacifier and plays with my chin. "Are you going to let yourself drift off to sleep? You look a little sleepy. Your mama said it's your naptime."

I glance up and find Maggie watching me soberly, and when I smile at her, her face softens into a smile.

Jesus, I want this with her. I want babies and a marriage. A *home*.

"You're awfully comfortable with a baby in your arms," Stasia says as she sits next to me and coos at Eve. "It's pretty damn cute."

"Damn!" Tommy announces, and Stasia hangs her head in shame. "Why? Why does he only say the bad words?"

"And now we have proof that it's not my fault," Kane says with a laugh, scooping up his son and kissing the boy's round cheek. "You can't be saying that, lad. It makes your mother a little nuts."

"Nuts," Tommy says, pointing at his mom.

"Not helping," Stasia informs her husband.

"Okay, everyone. Dinner's ready," Fiona announces as she walks into the living room, where we've all gathered. Her eyes grow misty, and she reaches for Tom's hand. "And isn't this a fine bunch? All of our loves together."

"Ma's getting sentimental," Shawn warns and stands to make a beeline for the dining room. "Let's go eat. I'm starving."

"Thanks for bringing the cake, Anastasia," Fiona says to her daughter-in-law as she gets ready to cut the white cake with ornate flowers decorating the top. "It's just beautiful. Is this the sort of thing you'll be selling in your new bakery?"

"On a smaller scale," Stasia confirms. "No more wedding cakes for me because they take too much time. We're getting close to opening. Just a few weeks left. We've decided to call it O'Callaghan's Bakery."

Tom's head comes up in surprise. "You are?"

"We are," Kane says. "It's a fine name and carries some tradition with it."

"A fine name it is," Tom agrees. "What sorts of things will you be selling then?"

"We'll have some Irish baked goods that I've learned to make during our visits to Ireland, along with some traditional American things. And I took some advice and spoke with the diner. They said they'd like some pastries each morning, as well."

"I'll be first in line the day you open," Keegan says. "Congratulations to the two of you."

"Stasia," Fiona says as she cuts into the pretty cake. "This is pink on the inside."

My eyebrows rise. Maggie squeezes my hand, and Izzy and Keegan share a look. Keegan nods.

"Well, I confided in the girls a couple of weeks ago, but we wanted to give it a little more time before we announced to everyone. And then, Maggie was gone, and so much has been happening. Anyway," Izzy says, "I'm pregnant again. And, we just found out that it's a girl."

"Eve's going to be a big sister," Maeve says and jumps up to hug Keegan in excitement. "And, coincidentally, we just found out the sex of ours a couple of days ago. The little stinker has been shy in our last few scans. It's a boy!"

The amount of excited noise that this group of people can make is on a decibel similar to that of championship football Sunday.

More hugs, tears, and laughter are spread around.

"I get a brother!" Rachel exclaims and hugs Maeve. "He's going to be *so* cute. Can we make his room a race car theme?"

"We can make it whatever you want," Hunter says with a wink.

"So much good news," Fiona says and wipes her eyes, then reaches for more tissues. "So many blessings."

"We have more," Shawn adds, smiling proudly at his wife as he wraps his arm around her shoulders. "No babies for us, but Lexi finished her book, and it's already been optioned for a movie."

"Holy shit!" Maggie exclaims and makes a beeline for Lexi, who's already been swept up in hugs.

"Shit!" Tommy mimics.

"Oops." Maggie cringes. "Sorry. This is the best news. I want to read it."

"I'll send it to you," Lexi promises. "And being optioned isn't a guarantee of a movie, but it's pretty cool that it hasn't even been released yet, and the studio is already interested."

"Such a wonderful accomplishment," I say and kiss her cheek. "Good job, Lex."

Rachel brushes a tear from her cheek, and Maeve wraps her arm around the teenager. "What's wrong?"

"I'm supposed to study abroad next year in France. But with the new babies, and all of the things happening with the family, I don't want to go. Ma, I'll miss everything. I don't want to do that."

"We'll talk about it," Hunter says and eyes Brian, who just lost his smile for the first time since he arrived.

I suspect there are several reasons that Rachel is rethinking her studies in Europe.

"There's no law that says you can't stay home," Tom assures her as he takes her hand in his. Tom and Rachel have had a special bond since the day they met. "I think your grandma and I will be here more often, as well. We don't want to miss anything either."

"Oh, sure, we start having kids, and you're around more," Kane says.

"Of course. We have grandbabies," Fiona says. "And more on the way. Thank goodness the house is almost ready for you, Keegan. You can't squeeze much more into that apartment above the pub."

"Just one more month," Izzy says, crossing her fingers. "They're wrapping up some last-minute things, and then we should be able to move in. I can't wait. Not that I'm not grateful for the home we have."

"You need more space," Maeve assures her. "That's not being ungrateful."

Maggie walks over to me, takes the sleeping Eve from my arms, passes her to Lexi, and then sits in my lap.

God, I love having her in my arms, but this blatant display of affection is surprising, given that we're with literally every single person in her family.

"Cake?" Rachel asks and passes us each a slice.

"Thanks," Maggie says and takes a bite of the pink cake. "Good."

"Get a room," Stasia says from behind her hand, then winks at us. "Just kidding. I think you're super cute. Maeve, can I put Tommy down for a nap somewhere? He's falling asleep in his cake. It's been a busy day."

"Of course." Maeve leads Stasia and the baby down the hall.

"My phone's ringing," Maggie says with a frown and wiggles around, tugging her phone from her pocket. "Hello? Leo?"

She sits up and plugs her other ear, listening.

"Okay, that sounds great. Yep. Okay. Thank you so much. This is exciting. Perfect, thank you."

She hangs up, turns to me, and bites her lip.

"What is it?"

"He just emailed me the finished song. I get to listen to it."

CHAPTER 16

~MAGGIE~

"What song?" Kane asks, and I turn to find everyone quiet and staring at me. Even Maeve and Stasia, who just walked back into the room.

"Oh, uh. Well, it's a long story."

"And we have all evening," Da says with a small smile. "What's going on, then?"

Cameron squeezes my shoulders, and I pull myself out of his lap, clearing my throat.

"So, I've been recording short songs and posting them on social media. It started as a little hobby because I like to sing, and the acoustics in my bathroom are pretty great. Anyway, in less than a year, I've grown to just over three million followers."

"What?" Maeve demands, reaching for her phone. "Mary Margaret, why didn't you tell us?"

"It's just a little—"

"Hobby," Shawn finishes and crosses his arms over his chest.

"Right. Anyway, Cam accidentally found out about it, and then he called Leo and surprised me with a recording day in the studio with Nash."

"This is *incredible*," Stasia says and dances a little jig. "Leo's the best. And *you're* the best. Let's listen to the song."

"Wait, you guys know Leo Nash?" Brian asks Rachel. "That's, like, *really* cool."

I swallow hard and look over at Cameron.

"Share it with them. It's beautiful."

"You've heard it?" Lexi asks.

"Just the rough cut," I explain. "But it's been remastered now. This is the final version. For the album—and the radio."

"The freaking *radio*?" Izzy demands. "They're releasing the single?"

"Yes. I think it's going to be the first single off the album."

"This is the coolest thing *ever*," Rachel says, bouncing in her seat. "Play it."

"We have to hear it," Maeve agrees. "Now. I'm dying here."

"Okay." Butterflies invade my stomach as I open my email.

"Wait," Hunter says, holding up a hand. "Not there. We need to listen to this the right way. We can tether your phone to my sound system."

"Excellent idea," Cam says and reaches for my cell. Within seconds, the two men have it connected through Bluetooth to the speakers that are all over the house. "Ready?"

"Oh, God, I'm going to hyperventilate," I mutter and wipe my hand down my face. "Okay. Hit play."

Cam kisses my forehead and leans over to whisper in my ear. "Don't worry, it's fantastic. They're already so proud of you."

With the tap of Cam's thumb on my phone screen, the room fills with music. Piano, followed by the addition of guitar, and then Leo's voice.

I join him at the chorus, and everyone around me smiles widely. The song builds through the second chorus, just me, and then the bridge.

It's such a beautiful song, and Leo was right. It's fantastic.

"Again," Da says when it ends, and Cam presses play once more. Halfway through, Maeve and Shawn are singing along, and by the end of it, I'm swept up in hugs and love, and we're back to celebrating again.

"I can't believe you didn't tell me," Maeve says.

"I've been a little busy," I remind her. "It's good, isn't it?"

"I'm going to give you a very honest opinion," Hunter says, his face completely sober. Oh, no. My stomach falls to my feet. But then, he grins. "It's freaking *amazing*. It's going to be a hit. I guarantee it."

"Tell them the rest," Cam urges.

"There's more?" Kane asks.

"Well, nothing set in stone. Leo just mentioned that maybe, if I'm interested, I could work as a backup singer for them on their next tour."

Again, silence fills the room.

"You're kidding," Shawn says at last.

"No, but again, it's just an idea. And only if I want to. It's a long way off, anyway."

Da wraps his arms around me and holds me close. "I'm so proud of you, baby girl."

"I NEED A GUINNESS, two whiskeys—neat—and a cola," I say to Keegan the following night. The pub is busy, and things are finally back to normal around here. I didn't realize how much I'd missed working at the pub until I was away for several days.

"You're a bossy one," Keegan says with a wink.

"You missed me. Oh, and there's a table in the back I'm keeping my eye on. College kids here for the weekend. They haven't been too bad, but the one on the end looks like he's gonna get handsy."

"I'll keep an eye out, too," Cam says from his seat next to me at the bar.

"If you're going to keep acting as security, you should get a polo shirt and a salary," I inform him. "I'm fine."

"I'm just making sure," he replies and sips his beer.

I like having him here. I especially love it when I glance his way and find him looking at me with those blue eyes that make me all gooey inside.

And then I remember the way he fucked me bent over the kitchen counter just this afternoon, and I have to fan myself with my notepad.

"Earth to Mary Margaret," Maeve says, waving a hand in front of my face. "You awake?"

"Sorry, yeah. What's up?"

"Your college kids are waving you down. I'm still not convinced that one in the corner is of age."

"He has an ID that says he's twenty-one," I reply with a shrug. "Doesn't look fake."

"If he's old enough to shave, I'm Julia Roberts."

"Okay, Julia, I'm off to make my rounds." I wink at her, but before I can turn away, the phone behind the bar rings, and Keegan grabs it. Since it *never* rings, we all pause to hear who it is.

"And a happy day it is to hear from you, Cousin Sinead," Keegan says with a smile. "It's early there, isn't it? Oh, aye."

My brother's accent kicks up a notch whenever he's in Ireland or around anyone else with the same accent.

Maeve and I share a look.

"I'll ask the family, of course. It's two weeks, then? We'll help you figure it out. I'll call you in the morning. Take care now."

Keegan hangs up and we all wait expectantly.

"What's up in Ireland?" I ask.

"Sinead needs help. One of her employees just quit because she got married and moved to the village over, and another broke her ankle, so she can't be on her feet. Sinead is wondering if we know of anyone over there to call. She's exhausted all of the contacts she has and just wanted some fresh ideas. It's a small village, you know."

"I'll go," I say immediately, the idea taking shape in my head. "I don't know what kind of help she needs, but I can do it. I've been wanting to go to Ireland for a while. It'll be a nice change of scenery. Can you spare me?"

"We have Ma and Rachel," Maeve says.

"They only need help for a couple of weeks," Keegan adds, thinking it over. "I should be able to get by without you for that long."

"Awesome." I clap my hands and turn to Cam. "You can go, right? You can work from anywhere."

"I wondered if I was invited," he says with a grin. "Yes, I can manage that."

"Awesome. I'll call Sinead myself and let her know." I sashay away, already excited by the thought of spending a couple of weeks across the pond, soaking in the air and listening to the music in the pubs.

The little inn that the family owns has the best views of the sea, and there are castle ruins nearby.

I can't wait.

"Hey, lady," the kid with the probable fake ID calls from across the room.

"Back to work for me," I say as I load my tray with the drink order and make my way to the customers. "Here you go, lads. Do you want to order any food?"

"Nachos," one says. "And maybe we should share some onion rings."

"Junk food it is, then." I wink and turn away just as the band starts playing one of my favorite songs. I swing over and sing with them as I make my way to the kitchen to place the food order.

I'm going to *Ireland.*

IT'S LATE, half-past three, when I walk into my house. I spent some time on the phone with Sinead after we closed, and I wanted to get ahead on some inventory work because Cam and I will have to leave for Ireland in just two days.

I could have gone to Cam's house after work, but I'm sure he's asleep by now. Instead, I came here, to my little house that I don't love, but which suits me just fine.

At least, the stench from the rotten food is gone.

I swing through the kitchen and set a kettle of water on the stove to boil for tea before walking back to the bedroom. I flip on the light and yelp. "Cam!"

"You're home."

"Why are you lurking in the dark?"

"I'm not *lurking.*" He laughs and stands before

crossing to me. He's in sweatpants and no shirt—muscles on full, glorious display.

"I knew you'd come here rather than my place," he says and rubs his hands up and down my arms. "I didn't know when you'd be back, so I came to bed."

"Did I wake you?"

"No." He kisses my forehead just as the kettle starts to whistle. "Let's go make your tea."

"I'm gonna change really quick," I inform him. "Right behind you."

"Take your time," he replies as he walks toward the kitchen.

Okay, I'm glad he's here. I don't like sleeping without him. I end up tossing and turning. And why shouldn't I be with him, when he's clearly more than happy to sleep with me?

I change into more comfortable clothes and then join Cam in the kitchen.

He's already poured the water and dunked my favorite tea in it.

"You're handy to have around," I inform him as I sit on a stool. "Thanks."

"Oh, you want some, too? This is mine." He grins and slides the hot mug across the island to me. "Just kidding. How was the rest of your night?"

"Pretty uneventful, actually. Steady, but nothing remarkable happened. I'm glad the college kids turned out to be harmless. I talked with Sinead before I came home."

I blow on the tea and take a sip.

"What's the plan?" he asks.

"First of all, are you okay with this? I made the decision without even talking with you about it first."

"You want to go, so we'll go. It's fine with me."

I nod in relief. "Great. I'm excited. We need to leave in two days. I know that's fast, but Sinead is really in a bind. Both of her housekeeping girls are out, and she needs help with breakfast in the morning. She's putting us up in the guest house on the property."

"Great," he says. "It'll be nice to be there."

"I think so, too." I sip my tea. "I'm excited to spend some quality time near the ocean."

"Uh, babe? I hate to be the one to break this to you, but *we* live near the ocean."

"I know." I wrinkle my nose. "But the inn has views of the ocean, and we're going to be staying on the property."

He leans against the countertop and crosses his arms over his impressive chest. "Okay, I have a question for you. What does your dream home look like?"

"Huh?"

"Humor me."

I look down into my mug as a series of images move through my mind, and then I shrug. "I don't know. Small, I guess. Simple."

"That's not good enough. Give me specifics."

"This is silly."

"No, it's not silly. I want you to answer the question.

I want you to *tell me* what you want rather than brushing the question away."

"I guess I want a Craftsman home, near the water, with a garden. I want a gourmet kitchen and enough bedrooms that I can be the cool aunt and have all the kids come to stay with me. And I want to see the ocean from my bedroom."

He nods. "That sounds amazing. Now, why couldn't you just say that in the first place? Why do I *always* have to coax and pull information out of you?"

"You don't—"

"I do." He rubs his hand over his face. "Your music, what kind of car you want, hell, just about anything at all. If I ask for your opinion, for what *you* want, you brush me aside and say anything is fine. But it's not fine, damn it. I want you to tell me what you want because it's my mission in life to give it to you."

My mouth drops open.

"I suspect that this is something left over from before," he continues, "and you don't have to confirm or deny that, but I'm not your former husband. I won't shut you down, make you feel stupid, or disregard your feelings. I want you to have whatever you want."

"I'm not used to asking for it," I admit. "Of course, I want a beautiful beach house. But the one I have is—"

"If you say *fine*, I'll spank your gorgeous ass."

I bite my lip.

"Let's work on this, okay? Be honest with me. We

established a while ago that we don't lie, and we don't keep secrets, right?"

"Yeah." I sigh and take another sip of tea. "I'll work on it."

"Good." He pushes away from the counter and walks around to me. "Now, let's go to bed so I can lose myself in you for a while."

"That sounds nice."

"I'm going for better than *nice*, sweetheart."

CHAPTER 17

"*I* can't sleep," I say and look over at Cam, who's watching me in the moonlight. "I should be *so tired* because we've done nothing but scramble for the last two days to get ready for this trip, but I'm all worked up and can't just lie in this bed anymore."

"Okay," he says and sits up, rubbing his hands over his face. "What do you want to do?"

"Can we go to the beach?"

He's quiet, and then he nods. "Sure. It's dark, so we won't be able to see much, but why not?"

We climb out of bed, quickly dress in layers because it'll be chilly out by the water, and then we're in my car, driving over to the beach's public access. I cut the engine, and Cam and I walk hand in hand to the sand.

"We can see the whitecaps on the waves," I point out. "They glow in the moonlight."

"It's pretty, even at three in the morning," he agrees and leads me to a washed-up log, where we sit and listen to the music of the ocean.

"I used to come down here," he says after a moment, "when I was a teenager, and my dad was passed-out drunk. I *hated* my home life, Mags. I hated that my mom left when I was young and didn't tell me why. No one ever explained it to me. One day, she was just gone. And for a long time, I used to wonder what I did wrong to chase her away."

I lay my cheek on his shoulder. "It wasn't your fault. You know that, right?"

"Now I do, yeah. Some parents just shouldn't *be* parents, and I get that it wasn't anything I did that made her leave. But it messed me up a bit. And then I started hanging out with Kane more and more, spent time at your house, and I saw what a family was supposed to look like. At first, I resented it. I was totally jealous of what Kane had with all of you, but you know how your parents just swallow you up and include you in everything, whether you like it or not?"

I laugh, thinking of what I said to Heather. "Oh, yeah, I get it."

"One day, I forgot to be jealous and just accepted that I was part of the family. I spent less time at home. And, frankly, I don't think my dad even noticed much. It was probably a relief to him. And then, I went away to the Army because I needed the structure. I needed to feel as if I belonged somewhere, and I knew that I wouldn't be able to afford college on my own."

"Did you like being in the Army?" I ask him.

"Yeah, I did. I liked the guys I served with, and when I found out that computers were my jam, and they put me through school for it, I was grateful again. I went from being in a shitty situation to having an opportunity to break that cycle. And I held on to it with both hands. Then chose a field that gives me a comfortable lifestyle. But it has its trade-offs."

"You can't talk about it," I whisper.

"That's the biggest one," he admits. "It's not that I'm a gossip, you know? I've never been one to offer up a bunch of information that isn't somebody's business. But it's not easy to have this huge job that literally *no one* can know about. No matter how much I trust someone or love them, I can't tell them what I have going on. I've signed agreements that state I can be incarcerated if I break that promise."

"I'm sorry that I gave you so much crap for always being so secretive and for not being around," I say, cupping his cheek in my palm. "I guess I'm selfish. I *want* to know because I care about you, and I want to know everything that you have going on. Not because I'm nosy."

"I get that. It's a simple, *'Hey, honey, how was your day?'* But I can't tell you about my day most of the time. And I hate that part of it. If I'd known, way back when,

225

that this was how it would be, I'm not so sure I'd do it again."

I frown and notice that the sky is starting to lighten with the early signs of dawn. "My da always says that if you change what happened before, the now would be different, too. And I wouldn't change this moment with you, Cam. I wouldn't wish this away."

"Me, either."

"I promise you I won't get angry about your job. When you have to be vague, or if you can't say anything at all, I won't hold it against you."

He kisses my forehead and takes a long, deep breath. "Thank you. I would never do anything to make you lose your trust in me. Just always remember that."

"I know you wouldn't. I *do* trust you. How could I not, after everything we've been through?"

We're quiet again, listening to the waves and watching as the day awakens.

"I always wanted to live on the water," I say to him, surprised that I'm confessing this for the first time out loud. "When Joey and I were looking for a house, I said I wanted to be close to the ocean, and he scoffed. Said we couldn't afford it, and even if we could, a house exposed to the elements and salt water would require too much maintenance. Of course, I didn't know that he had a whole slew of money hidden away.

"I feel more alive when the sea is in view than I do at any other time in my life. It's like it fuels my soul somehow, you know? It rejuvenates me. And I can picture myself with a little vegetable garden so I can grow food to put in my recipes. Of course, there's a dog sleeping in the sunshine, and maybe a swing set in the yard."

I swallow hard and then take a shaky breath.

"I've never told anyone that before. I'd stopped daydreaming about those things."

"I think you should start again, Mary Margaret," Cam says and wraps his arm around my shoulders. "I like that particular daydream."

"I do, too." God, have I ever felt so content? So at ease? I don't think I've trusted anyone the way I do Cam. I know that I could open my soul to him, the way I just did, and I would be safe.

And that's more than love.

That's everything.

"Cam, are you about ready?" I call up the stairs at his house. Our flight leaves in four hours, and with a ferry ride ahead of us, we need to get a move on. But there's no answer. "Cam?"

I could have sworn I just heard him up there.

I climb the stairs and check his bedroom, but it's empty. I swing around to his office, but he's not in there, either. He was just here, though, because his computer is on, and his email lights the screen.

"Cam?"

I turn to leave, but then a single word on the computer screen catches my eye.

Lemon.

I know, deep in my heart, that I have no business looking at this email, but before I can talk myself out of it, I take a step closer.

I need you back on the Lemon case. New information has come to light that I know you can dig deeper on. Similar to five years ago in the Caymans. Call me.

-R

"Sorry, I had to go grab a bag—" Cam's voice trails off when he sees me looking at the computer screen. His eyes narrow. "Maggie."

"Don't you *dare* Maggie me." I prop my hands on my hips. "Tell me this isn't about my late husband."

"It must not have gone to sleep when I told it to."

"I don't *care* about that," I reply and feel my heart stop. "Tell me this isn't about Joey."

"I can't tell you that." His voice is as flat as his blue eyes, which are now emotionless.

"Tell me what this is about."

"I can't do that, either. You *know* I can't."

"Cameron." My heart is pounding in double-time now. "Damn it, say *something*. You're the one who reminded me just this morning that we don't keep secrets, damn it. That you'd never keep something from me that would hurt me."

"I can't talk about this. I'm sorry, Mags, but I can't."

"You're sorry." I nod slowly. "You had information

about my husband *five fucking years ago*, and you didn't tell me about it. You know what you are, Cam? You're a hypocrite."

"Maggie, just stop it." His voice is hard. Angry. "We just talked about this *hours* ago. You know I can't tell you what I know, even if every fiber in me *screams* to talk about it. I can't. I'm no hypocrite. I'm doing my fucking job."

I shake my head in denial. Of course, I can accept his job when it involves *strangers.* But when it's about my husband? About *me*?

And then it hits me.

"Wait. If you were investigating Joey, you were investigating *me.*"

His jaw clenches, but he doesn't say anything at all.

"*Cameron!*"

"I. Can't. Talk. About. It."

"Fine, I'm out of here." I hurry past him and jog down the steps. "I have a plane to catch, and I don't want you to go."

"Good," he says stiffly. Tears threaten, but I'll be damned if I shed a single one with him watching. "I think, given the circumstances, it's time for a break. Maybe this isn't what I thought it was, Mary Margaret."

"Right. Great." I grab my purse and walk out the door to my car with my bag already in the back. Then, I drive away from Cam's house. I have a plane to Ireland to catch.

"Damn it." I slap the steering wheel as I drive

toward the ferry. "He's been lying to me for years. He knew about the Caymans all along. How could he do this to me?"

With tears on my cheeks, I drive my SUV onto the ferry and take a long, deep breath.

I'm going without him.

CHAPTER 18

~CAMERON~

*K*eegan turns to me with a smile, and then that smile disappears when recognition dawns. "I thought you were going to Ireland with Maggie three days ago."

I shake my head. "No. I didn't go. I'm gonna need a beer, please."

The other man's eyes narrow on me, but he reaches for a clean glass and builds me a Guinness, just as Tom walks over and claps me on the shoulder.

"What are you doing here, lad? You're supposed to be with my Maggie."

Just keep cutting my heart out, why don't you? I knew better than to come into the pub.

"I didn't go," I reply shortly and sip the beer.

The two men are quiet, and then Keegan gets pulled away to help another customer.

"Shall we talk about it, then?" Tom asks simply and climbs onto the stool next to mine.

God, I've been dreading this. I'm an idiot. I never should have started something with her. I knew if it fell apart, it'd change everything between the entire fucking family and me. And that hurts almost as much as losing Maggie.

"Are you just going to drink?" Tom asks.

"I don't honestly know what to say," I reply at last.

"I've always found the best place to start is the beginning."

After another sip, I tap my fingers on the glass, lift it, and gesture for Tom to join me at one of the booths in the corner, where it's a bit more private.

Once we're seated, I take a deep breath.

"Before I tell you any of this, I need you to know that it can never be repeated."

"You can trust me. Hell, I'm your father in every way that counts, boy." And by the look on his face, he's offended that I even have to question his integrity.

"I know." I swallow hard. "I know it. But I still have to say it because I'm not supposed to say what I'm about to. But, damn it, I need to talk to you. Five years ago, I was brought in on a case at work. One that involved your former son-in-law and the woman I'm in love with. A money laundering case."

I can't tell him everything, but I skim through the story.

"Eventually, I had to take myself off the case

because it became a conflict of interest for me. How could I do that? How could I investigate people I love more than anything? I couldn't, so I pulled back. But not before I knew just about everything there was to know. And, of course, because of the nature of my job, I couldn't talk to Maggie about it. Not back then, not when Joey died, and not now."

"You told me," he points out.

"I've only barely scratched the surface. I can't tell you anything else, and I'm sure you have questions, but I can't answer them."

"Okay, then."

Two words, so easily given that it almost takes my breath away.

"Well, the morning we were supposed to go to Ireland, Maggie saw an email on my computer from my former boss, telling me that they need me for more on the Lemon case. It didn't give any specific information, but she saw enough."

"And she was angry," Tom correctly guesses.

"Oh, yeah," I agree. "And, honestly, I got mad, too. We'd just had this great conversation the night before, and she'd assured me that she understood about my job and that she wouldn't be mad or pressure me to talk about it. And then she saw the damn email, and everything she promised went right out the window."

"Of course, it did," Tom says. "It was about her husband, not a stranger."

"I get that." I rub my hands over my face. I'm

fucking exhausted. I haven't slept in days. "She went to Ireland without me after I said we needed a break. We both said things that we'll likely regret later. Hell, I regret it now. But at the root of it all, despite having the best of intentions and wanting to be supportive, I'm not convinced that Maggie will ever be able to truly accept my job and the secrets I have to keep from her."

The other man sits back in the booth and studies me for a long moment. And then, to my utter surprise, he says, "Bollocks."

"I know, I shouldn't have talked to you about this. She's your daughter, and I messed up. I'll apologize to her and wish her the best—"

"Is it a punch in the bloody face you're looking for, then?"

I frown at him. "Uh, no."

"Then shut up and listen. I haven't heard you say anything that tells me that what's happened can't be fixed. Yes, you need to apologize, but from the sound of it, my daughter has an apology to make, as well. You don't go through any relationship without some rough patches, and that's the truth of it. Why, my Fiona is a saint and an angel, but there has been many a day that I wanted to wring her pretty little neck."

"But you two get along so well. You never fight."

He busts up into laughter. "Of course, we fight. We've had some big rows over the years, and there might have been a night or two that I slept on the couch. But that didn't mean we politely went our separate ways. You might as well tear my beating heart out of my chest by simply suggesting it. You don't throw away the love of your life over a misunderstanding."

I sip my beer, considering him.

"You'll fight. You'll be angry and hurt and so frustrated you can hardly see straight. And then you'll make up and love each other, and the bad times will pass you by—just like the good ones do."

"It's not that I'm throwing our relationship away," I say slowly. "I can't see my life without her. But I also can't get the image of the look on her face out of my mind. That moment after she saw the email. That look of *betrayal* has haunted me for days, and I feel like my hands are tied because I can't confide in her about what happens at the job, even if it pertains to her family. And that tells me that I'll never have her trust. Not fully."

"I think you're doing a lot of assuming," Tom replies. "If I were you, I'd get my arse on a plane to Ireland and have it out with her until you see eye to eye and can work past it. Staying here and pouting isn't going to solve anything."

"I'm not pouting."

"Aren't you?" He laughs, shakes his head, and raps his knuckles on the table. "Looks that way to me. My money's on you, lad. It always has been."

He walks behind the bar to help Keegan tend to customers, and I push my mostly full beer away, no longer interested in it.

I'll check Maggie's house on my way home, just to make sure that everything is as it should be, and then lose myself in work.

The way I always do.

THREE DAYS LATER, with Def Leppard pounding in my ears, I'm punching the hell out of a bag in Hunter's gym. He's always given the family full access to the facilities whenever we want to work out, and since I still can't sleep well, I decided to come here and punch something that doesn't bleed or punch back.

After twenty minutes, when I'm a sweaty mess, I turn to reach for a towel on my way to the treadmill, where I plan to run for a while.

But when I turn, someone's behind me.

And in the almost dark, I almost swore it was Maggie.

"Good morning," Maeve says.

"Sorry, I didn't see you," I say after pulling one earbud out of my ear and letting it fall over my shoulder. "Did I wake you when I shut my car door?"

"No, I was awake," she says and pats her belly. I swear, it's grown in the week since I last saw her. "This little one seems to like being active mostly at night. It's the weirdest feeling, having a little *thing* tumbling around inside of you, kicking your ribs and kidneys."

"Does it hurt?"

"Not yet. I've been told that in another month or so it will, so I'm not really complaining. I just miss a good night's sleep."

"I understand that."

She's quiet as I unravel the tape from my hands and then finally look over at her. "What's on your mind?"

"Who says anything is on my mind?" she counters. "Maybe I just wanted to come out here and watch you work out."

"You've never been a good liar." I toss the used tape into the trash and wipe the sweat off my face with the towel. "Go ahead, yell at me."

"I don't want to yell at you. Don't get me wrong, I *did* want to a few days ago. But now, I just want to hug you."

And so she does. Just wraps her arms around me and presses that round belly against me, holding me close.

It feels nice.

"My sister is a pain in the ass a lot," she says as she pulls away. "She has a quick temper, and she doesn't always listen when you need her to. But I know she loves you, even if she hasn't said the words. Have you thought about going to Ireland?"

"No." My voice is gruff, even to my ears. "I thought I'd wait until she gets home to try to talk to her."

"Why? You're miserable."

"I told her we needed a break, and I'm giving her one."

"To what end? So you can both spend the next week absolutely miserable?"

"She's miserable?" I ask, my head coming up fast. "Have you spoken with her?"

"Not really. She doesn't want to talk about it, and I know she's been busy at the inn. But a sister knows these things. She's been gone for almost a week, and you've both had time to calm down and work your way to the lonely and regretful part of things. If you miss her, if you want to see her, don't be a stubborn ass. Just go get her already."

I frown down at my hands.

I already considered that late last night as I lay in my cold bed, pining for Maggie.

It's ridiculous. I'm a grown man. What am I waiting for?

"Thanks, Maeve." I kiss her cheek and then head for the door. "I have some arrangements to make."

"Good. What is it with you two always dragging your feet? Just love each other already."

I laugh for the first time in days as I hurry out to my car. I have to book the next flight and get ready to go.

I open my phone and bring up Maggie's number and start to type a message.

But what am I going to say? *Hey, I'm coming to see you. I miss you. Don't reject me.*

Nope, not gonna do that.

So, instead, I erase the text and get started making

arrangements to get off this island and to the one the love of my life is currently standing on.

I'm sick of fighting myself and being without her. It's time to be honest and tell Maggie what I want, what I need, and get the same from her.

The truth.

And, even if I have to break my contract, I'll tell her what she needs to know to get her back. She's the most important thing in my life. I've been absolutely lost without her since the minute she walked out of my house. I wanted to run after her then, but I was too hurt. Too stubborn. That stops now.

I'll be damned if Joey Lemon—or anyone else—will keep me from her.

CHAPTER 19

~MAGGIE~

"Can I get you some more coffee, Mr. Dugan?" I ask the elderly man who isn't actually an overnight guest of the inn. Still, he comes in for coffee and a full Irish breakfast, which consists of enough food to feed a family of four, three times a week. Sinead told me that she doesn't even charge him because he lost his wife last year, and this gets him some company. He's a sweet man, and he enjoys chatting with the guests, asking them questions about where they come from and then giving information about the area.

He should be a tour guide.

"Aye, thank you, lass." He holds up his mug for me and smiles gratefully. "You're a lovely sight to see first thing in the morning, sweet Maggie."

"Thank you, Mr. Dugan. And you're as handsome as

can be. Just wave me over if you need more coffee, you hear?"

I've been working hard, day and night since I arrived a week ago. I can't complain, as I knew I was here for work, and it helps to keep my mind off a certain American back home.

"I've got the dining room covered," Sinead says when I walk back to the kitchen for a fresh pot of coffee. "Now that the biscuits are out of the oven, do you mind seeing to the laundry upstairs? Guests should be checking out soon, and then we can get started on cleaning the rooms."

"Sure thing."

"Maggie." Sinead, a pretty woman just a few years older than me with dark red hair and happy green eyes, looks concerned as she takes my hand in hers. "Are you all right? You've seemed so sad since the day you got here, and I didn't want to intrude. But it breaks my heart to see you this way day in and day out."

I sigh, wrinkling my nose. "Is it that obvious?"

"Only to me because I've known you for most of your life. I may not see you often, but I know you're usually much happier than this."

"There's a man back home." The comment is simple but says it all.

"Ah, and a man can surely bring out the sadness in a woman, can't he? I'm going to the pub tonight for a pint and some food that I don't have to make myself. Why don't you join me?"

I immediately start to decline. After all, I'm not a ton of fun right now, but then I reconsider. Why should I be sad and mopey the whole time I'm in Ireland?

"You know, that sounds like a lot of fun. What time should I be ready?"

"By five. Excellent." Sinead smiles and pats my shoulder, then leaves the kitchen with a tray of biscuits for the customers.

The workday runs smoothly and quickly, given that we only had four couples check out today. I'm all finished with my duties by early afternoon, so after a quick change of clothes, I grab my windbreaker and a hat and set off for the cliffs.

The salty sea air is a welcome thing as I make my way over the green grass to the cliffs and just stand, breathing in the air and watching the waves.

Yes, this is my happy place. I could stand here forever.

The truth is, I've been angry *and* sad this week. Confused. And then angry again.

Cam hasn't reached out even once. Last night, I picked up my phone, and when I brought our last texts up, I saw three dots as if he were typing something. I was so excited and nervous to hear from him, but then the dots disappeared, and there was nothing.

Not one thing in more than a week.

I have so many questions, and I know that he won't answer any of them.

And that's damn frustrating.

I make my way inland to the castle ruins that I played in and around as a child. I used to daydream about leprechauns and faeries running around, granting wishes. Once, I could have sworn I heard the music from long ago being played through the mists around the ruins, but I didn't tell anyone because they would have told me I was hearing things.

But if you can't think of such fanciful things in Ireland, then where can you?

There's an ancient cemetery behind the ruins with stones long ago weathered, so the names aren't readable. But I think it's a beautiful place. Every day after I finish work, I come walk out this way, listen to the waves crashing against the cliffs, and sing softly to myself.

I haven't posted on social media in more than a week.

I've unplugged, as they say. And although I miss Cam something terrible, it's been nice to be here, working hard and letting the sea soothe my bruised heart.

I check the time and realize that I need to head back to the guest house so I can get ready to go to the pub with Sinead. I haven't been yet, and it'll be fun to run into locals that know my family, sing, and listen to the old-timers tell tall tales.

For one evening, I'll forget that I'm homesick. Not for a place but for a man.

~

"I ALWAYS HAD such a crush on your brother Kane," Shannon O'Dwyer says with a laugh as she sets my fish and chips in front of me. "And still do, if I'm being honest. But his wife is a sweetheart, and I did just fine with my Danny. How's your family, Maggie?"

"They're all doing well," I reply. "More babies are on the way, and my parents couldn't be happier."

"Well, isn't that fine, then?" Shannon says with a wink. "Would you like another pint?"

"Sure, why not?"

"Be right up," she says and hurries off with her tray lofted in the air.

"Why don't you get up there and sing, Maggie?" Another cousin, Shaemus, says from across the hightop table. "We'd all love to listen."

"Maybe after another pint," I say with a wink. "And you'll have to do it with me."

"Deal."

"Excuse me, Mary Margaret."

I look up into Finn O'Leary's cornflower-blue eyes and smile.

"Hi, Finn."

He rests his hand on my shoulder and leans in for a chat so we can hear each other well over the music that just started. "I'd like the chance to take you out while you're here. If you're agreeable to it."

"Oh, I—"

"You're going to want to take your hand off her."

The voice I've wanted to hear for a week comes through loud and clear. But as Finn starts to move away, I take his hand and plant it back on my shoulder.

Cam's eyes narrow.

I glare right back at him.

"You don't get to just walk in here and dictate who can and can't touch me, Cameron Cox."

Stop this. You're happy to see him! Jump into his arms and tell him you're sorry for saying horrible things.

"It's okay, Maggie, I'll just go sit—"

"You'll stay," I say to poor Finn and then turn back to Cam. "You don't get to be bossy. You haven't even *called* me since I got here. How did you know I was here, anyway?"

"I stopped by the inn first," he says, calm as can be. "They told me where to find you."

Finn tries to move away again, but I grab his wrist and narrow my eyes at him.

"If you know what's good for you, Finn O'Leary, you'll keep your hand right there."

"You might want to listen to her, Finn," Sinead says with a distinct laugh in her voice.

"I should have called," Cam begins.

"You won't get an argument from me. You should have called. You should have just talked to me when I was there so we could have hashed it all out right then and there. But no. You were pigheaded, and…Finn, I'm warning you."

"C'mon, Maggie," Finn mutters and then shakes his head woefully.

"Are you done yet?" Cam asks.

"I beg your pardon?"

"If you're done with your little tirade, I'll tell you that I'm madly in love with you and I'm here to make things right."

I blink at him, then look over at Finn. "Okay, you can let go now, Finn."

"Thank God," Finn says and scurries away.

"Come with me," Cam says as he takes my hand and leads me through the crowd in the pub, all of who are watching us now. We exit through a door to the outside. It's cool outside, with a thick, heavy fog hanging, casting everything in shadow.

"We can go to my place," I begin, but he frames my face with his hands and stares down at me longingly as though he hasn't seen me in years. "Cam."

"I love you, Mary Margaret. And I know that we have stuff to talk about, but damn it, I can't go another day without telling you that."

"I love you, too."

He blinks as if he's completely surprised.

"Why does that shock you? Why do you think I was so frustrated and angry?"

"Because of Joey—"

"No, not because of Joey. Because of *you*. And we can talk about this later because I really need you to kiss me—"

His mouth is on mine, not moving, just resting as if he's relieved to be here finally. And then, with those hands cupping my face, he sinks into me in that amazing way Cam does that makes my toes curl.

"I'm staying in the guest house," I inform him when he pulls away. "It's private."

"Let's go there," he suggests, not in a firm, stern way, but in a hopeful manner that makes me smile.

"If it will get us out of the cold, damp air, I'm all for it," I say with a smile and walk with him to his car. I give him directions to the inn and the small guest house behind it, and once he's parked and we're inside, I light the peat fire to warm us and turn to find him staring at me with hungry blue eyes.

"First," he begins, "I called my former boss and told him that I won't be helping out on that case due to a severe conflict of interest. I can't give you specific details, but I can say that I did the same several years ago for the same reasons."

"But you already knew most of what there was to know," I guess and can see on his face that I'm right.

"I understand your anger," he says. "Hell, I'd be mad, too."

"I promised you that I wouldn't be angry or hold your job against you. Of course, I didn't realize that this was part of that job, but I made the promise all the same, and my reaction that morning wasn't the caring and supportive person that you need. I'm sorry for that."

"And I'm sorry that I can't tell you everything. However, I will say that you now know everything that I knew. I'm not withholding intel that you don't have. I promise you that."

"Intel." I grin at him. "It's sexy when you sound all smart and stuff."

His shoulders sag as if he's incredibly relieved. "Are we going to be okay, Mags?"

I cross to him and wrap my arms around his middle, pressing my ear to his chest.

"We're good. This past week, I discovered that I missed you more than I was mad at you. And it occurred to me that it makes sense that Joey was being investigated, what with all that money he had hidden away. I hope that you and your cohorts realized that I wasn't a part of it."

"We knew that," he assures me and kisses the top of my head. His hands slide up and down my back. "I missed you, too. I wanted to call you, but I told you we needed a break, so I figured we'd speak when you got home."

"Stubborn," I whisper. "Both of us are stubborn."

Cam tips my chin up and kisses me softly. Gently. And when I slide my hands up under his shirt, he groans.

"Where's the bedroom?" he asks gruffly.

"Through there." I gesture with my head toward the back of the house. Suddenly, I'm in Cam's arms, being carried to the bedroom and tenderly laid on the bed.

Our movements are swift, both of our clothes shed until we're finally skin to skin.

"I was homesick," I confess and cup his face in my hand. "But not for Washington. For *you*, Cam."

"Baby," he whispers and kisses my lips, nudging his way between my legs. "I'm right here, my love. I'm not going anywhere. Well, until you do. And I know, I promised this before, and I let you walk away because I was suddenly scared and stupid, and I'm sorry for that. But, I vow to not let either one of us just up and leave at the first damn hurdle. We're so much better than that."

I grin and then gasp when he slips inside of me, holds one of my hands over my head, and begins to move in long, steady strokes.

"You're mine, Mary Margaret." Those blue eyes are fierce now. "And I'm yours until the day I die."

Then, words are lost in the sighs and the moans of delight as I'm led back into the light and amazing comfort of being with Cam.

Six months later...

"Good God, there are *so many signatures*," I say with a sigh and sign my name for the fortieth time in less than twenty minutes. Maeve and the nice man from the title company both laugh at me.

Cam takes the paper I just signed and does the same next to my name.

"That's it," Maeve says and slides keys across the table to us. "It's all yours."

"Can we go there now?" I ask as excitement fizzes through me like bubbles in champagne.

"Absolutely, it's yours," Maeve says. "Congratulations."

"Let's go," Cam says, and we are all smiles as we get in his car, and he drives us from the middle of town to the cliffs that overlook the ocean. The song that I recorded with Leo comes on the radio, and with a grin, Cam turns up the volume.

This song has been sitting in the top twenty on the charts for the past month. It's absolutely insane to me. And, I agreed to tour with them on their North American dates later this year, but I don't want to tour for years on end. That's just not me.

My home is here, with my family.

"It's just so *pretty*," I breathe as Cam parks in our new driveway and I stare up at the house. "I mean, just look at it. Maeve did a good job with this one."

I hop out of the car and hurry up the steps of the porch, but Cam says behind me, "Stop. We can't go in yet."

I turn and frown at him. "We can't?"

"Not quite yet." He joins me, takes my hand, and leads me to the porch swing that wasn't here yesterday.

"Did you hang this?"

"Your brother and da did," he confirms. "I know you love your porch swing."

"I do." My eyes want to get misty. "That's the sweetest thing."

"Have a seat," he suggests. And when I do, he drops to one knee before me.

"Holy crap."

Cam chuckles and pulls a ring out of his pocket. "Before we go inside *our* new house, I want to do this out here first. Mary Margaret, you are everything I've never looked for. I feel like we've taken a long, twisty road to meet where we did, but I'm grateful. I don't know what I'd do without you in my life. You're kind, smart, hardworking. And, frankly, I even love your temper."

I reach out to brush my fingers down his cheek.

"Please marry me, Mags. Make a life, a *home* with me. I promise I'll never make you regret it."

"Of course, I'll marry you," I reply with a huge grin and then sigh when he puts the emerald on my finger. "Is this my grandma's ring?"

"Yes. Your ma gave it to me when I went to ask them for your hand. I know it's old-fashioned, but I wanted to do that."

"And I love that you did." I lean over and kiss his lips, then wrap my arms around his neck as he lifts me and carries me toward the door. He sets me down and then picks me up again, his arm under my knees and behind my back this time to carry me over the threshold.

Cam opens the door and steps inside into our new home, and I can see the ocean through the windows. But more than that, I can see our future here.

Our children.

Christmases and summer celebrations.

I see our life. And nothing has ever been so sweet.

EPILOGUE

~TOM O'CALLAGHAN~

Five Years Later

*I*t's a charmed life that I lead. I have the luck of the Irish in spades when it comes to my family. It's been that way since the day my sweet Fiona agreed to marry me and then gave me five beautiful children.

Now, those children are having babies of their own and fill my heart with so much joy and pride, it feels as though it might just burst with it.

"I have to go speak with my Rachel," I say to Fiona before kissing her on the cheek. "I have a wee something for her."

"Give her my love. I'll save your seat." My bride

winks at me before I leave the room and walk down the hallway to Rachel's room, where my Maeve is helping her daughter get ready for today.

"May I come in?" I ask after a soft knock on the door.

"Of course, you can, Grandda," Rachel says with a big smile.

As I take her in from tip to toe, I shake my head in absolute amazement. "It's a vision you are, my darlin' girl."

Maeve smiles and hugs me. "I'll see you both out there. Your dad will be here in a minute, Rach."

Rachel nods happily, and I gingerly hug my grand-daughter, not wanting to mess up her beautiful white dress.

From the moment I met her as a surly fifteen-year-old girl, I felt a connection with her. There's not a moment we share that our heads aren't together as we chat and plot. Rachel has a special little place in my heart, and she will until the day I'm no longer on this Earth.

"You're sure about this Brian?" I ask her with a smile, and she laughs.

"I've loved him since I was seventeen," she says.

"And you're only a woman of twenty-two."

"You were nineteen when you married Grandma. You said so yourself."

I nod, unable to argue. The truth is, I like this Brian,

but it feels as though he's taking my girl from me, and that makes me a wee bit sad.

"I wanted to give you this," I say and open my hand, revealing a brooch that belonged to my grandmother. "It's sapphires, so it's something blue. Belonged to my grandma, so your great-grandma, and I know she would have loved you very much. She'd want you to have this."

"Grandda," Rachel whispers and brushes her finger over the sparkling blue stones. "I'll pin it to my bouquet. It's so beautiful. But are you sure you don't want to give it to…well, to someone related by blood?"

I frown and take her sweet hand. "Darlin', you are my family by something just as strong as blood. You're my granddaughter of the heart, and I couldn't love you more. Couldn't be more *proud* of you. Your grandma and I have plenty of nice things to give to all of our grandchildren, and we chose this for you."

"Thank you," she whispers and then sniffles. "Okay, I don't want to ruin my makeup. It took an hour to get me like this."

"Brian's going to pass out, and that's the truth of it." I kiss her cheek and then turn to leave, just as Hunter comes to the door and almost passes out himself at his first look of his daughter.

"Wow," he says.

"It's a vision she is." I shake his hand and pat his shoulder. Walking your daughter down the aisle isn't an easy thing. "Good luck, my boy."

I walk out of the house to where the wedding ceremony has been set up, and Fiona waits for me to walk her to our seats.

"How is she?" she asks me.

"Gorgeous," I reply and kiss her cheek.

I offer her my arm, and we walk down the white aisle to our seats in the second row. I'm overcome with pride as I see my children, all seated with their spouses, the people who make *them* better, as well as their wonderful, perfect children.

Kane and Anastasia have their two babies. Kane has his arm around his wife and their youngest daughter on his lap.

Keegan and Izzy, with their three kids, sit beside them, and next to Izzy is our Lexi, holding one of Izzy's little ones with my handsome Shawn by her side.

My sweet Mary Margaret and the son of my heart, Cameron, sit on the end of the row, holding their newborn babe, Jude.

Fiona and I sit behind my sweet Maeve, and I catch Brian's gaze as he stands nervously, waiting for Rachel to join him. I send him a wink, and he does the same in return.

Yes, I like this boy.

Moments later, the wedding march plays, and we all stand to watch Hunter escort Rachel down the aisle.

Fiona grasps my hand tightly, and I know what she's thinking.

How lucky are we that we're here to witness our eldest granddaughter marry?

How lucky are we, indeed?

IF YOU LOVE the With Me In Seattle series, Kristen Proby has something all-new for you that you won't want to miss!

The Secret releases on March 22, 2022, and is available for preorder here: https://www. kristenprobyauthor.com/thesecret

From *NYT* and *USA Today* Bestselling author Kristen Proby comes a *forbidden romance*. *The Secret* is the first in the Single in Seattle series!

VAUGHN IS everything I'm supposed to stay away from. Sexy. Cocky. *And famous.*

Ultra-famous.

I grew up in a family full of wealthy celebrities. My father, Luke Williams, is *the* celebrity of them all. A superstar actor and producer, my father knows the downside of living in the spotlight. And because of that, he sheltered my siblings and me from everything Hollywood entailed. We didn't attend premieres. We weren't photographed. There were no friendships with other celebrities' children.

The limelight couldn't touch us.

But now, at twenty-five, I'm ready to start my life, working for my father's production company in downtown Seattle—until Vaughn Barrymore walks through the door.

He can't keep his hands off me. He's completely

forbidden, but I can't help falling for the sweet, complicated man.

When—and it's *when* not *if*—my family finds out that I've been keeping this secret, will I have to choose between the man I love and those who mean the most to me? Or, by some miracle, can I have both?

ALSO COMING in 2022 is Lighthouse Way, the first in the all-new Huckleberry Bay Series!

You can preorder here: https://www. kristenprobyauthor.com/lighthouse-way

FROM **NYT** BESTSELLING **Author Kristen Proby comes an all new epic series about three best friends, a local legend, and finding love on the stunning Oregon Coast!**

LUNA WINCHESTER'S life is firmly entrenched in the coastal town Huckleberry Bay, Oregon. A fourth-generation light keeper, Luna is carrying on the Winchester tradition by tending to the lighthouse. Plus, she's decided to renovate a long-abandoned building on the property and make it a B&B, Luna's Light. Surrounded by family and her two childhood best friends, her life is full.

. . .

WOLFE CONRAD IS IN HIDING, and he's come to Huckleberry Bay to heal. A career ending accident on the track nearly took his life, and now he seeks refuge to try and build a new one. The quaint town's slow pace rattles the man who's first love is fast cars—and then there's the beautiful innkeeper, who rattles him in different ways.

FALLING in love with Luna definitely isn't part of Wolfe's plan. Local legends that tell of unrequited love and despair? Unbelievable. But stranger things have happened, like two strangers falling in love...

ABOUT THE AUTHOR

Kristen Proby has published more than sixty titles, many of which have hit the USA Today, New York Times and Wall Street Journal Bestsellers lists.

Kristen and her husband, John, make their home in her hometown of Whitefish, Montana with their two cats and dog.

- facebook.com/booksbykristenproby
- instagram.com/kristenproby
- bookbub.com/profile/kristen-proby
- goodreads.com/kristenproby

NEWSLETTER SIGN UP

I hope you enjoyed reading this story as much as I enjoyed writing it! For upcoming book news, be sure to join my newsletter! I promise I will only send you news-filled mail, and none of the spam. You can sign up here:

https://mailchi.mp/kristenproby.com/newsletter-sign-up

Other Books by Kristen Proby

The With Me In Seattle Series

Come Away With Me
Under The Mistletoe With Me
Fight With Me
Play With Me
Rock With Me
Safe With Me
Tied With Me
Breathe With Me
Forever With Me
Stay With Me
Indulge With Me
Love With Me
Dance With Me

Dream With Me
You Belong With Me
Imagine With Me
Shine With Me
Escape With Me
Flirt With Me
Change With Me

Check out the full series here: https://www.
kristenprobyauthor.com/with-me-in-seattle

The Big Sky Universe

Love Under the Big Sky
Loving Cara
Seducing Lauren
Falling for Jillian
Saving Grace

The Big Sky
Charming Hannah
Kissing Jenna
Waiting for Willa
Soaring With Fallon

Big Sky Royal
Enchanting Sebastian
Enticing Liam
Taunting Callum

Heroes of Big Sky
Honor

Courage

Shelter

Check out the full Big Sky universe here: https://
www.kristenprobyauthor.com/under-the-big-sky

Bayou Magic
Shadows

Spells

Serendipity

Check out the full series here: https://www.
kristenprobyauthor.com/bayou-magic

The Romancing Manhattan Series

All the Way

All it Takes

After All

Check out the full series here: https://www.
kristenprobyauthor.com/romancing-manhattan

The Boudreaux Series

Easy Love

Easy Charm

Easy Melody

Easy Kisses

Easy Magic

Easy Fortune

Easy Nights

Check out the full series here: https://www.kristenprobyauthor.com/boudreaux

The Fusion Series

Listen to Me

Close to You

Blush for Me

The Beauty of Us

Savor You

Check out the full series here: https://www.kristenprobyauthor.com/fusion

From 1001 Dark Nights

Easy With You

Easy For Keeps

No Reservations

Tempting Brooke

Wonder With Me

Shine With Me

Kristen Proby's Crossover Collection

Soaring with Fallon, A Big Sky Novel

Wicked Force: A Wicked Horse Vegas/Big Sky Novella
By Sawyer Bennett

All Stars Fall: A Seaside Pictures/Big Sky Novella
By Rachel Van Dyken

Hold On: A Play On/Big Sky Novella
By Samantha Young

Worth Fighting For: A Warrior Fight Club/Big Sky
Novella
By Laura Kaye

Crazy Imperfect Love: A Dirty Dicks/Big Sky Novella
By K.L. Grayson

Nothing Without You: A Forever Yours/Big Sky
Novella
By Monica Murphy

Check out the entire Crossover Collection here:
https://www.kristenprobyauthor.com/kristen-proby-
crossover-collection

CPSIA information can be obtained
at www.ICGtesting.com
Printed in the USA
LVHW090730120222
710987LV00005B/205